Reeve's voice was unexpectedly soft

His fingers touched her hair, slipping her headband free from her head. "There ought to be a law against confining hair like yours." He ran long brown hands across the shining honey-gold strands, stroking the hair away from her face, letting it slide through his fingers until it floated free in the breeze. "It wants to be free," Reeve whispered.

Marion quivered under his touch. "So do I," she choked, suddenly frightened of the fires that were kindled by his touch, frightened that he might sense them. But she could not move. Just like the hare that earlier had been crouching beneath the shadow of Reeve's helicopter, she was rooted to the ground.

"Do you, Marion?" Reeve questioned softly, his eyes raking her face. "I wonder...."

Shadow of an Eagle

by

SUE PETERS

Harlequin Books

TORONTO·LONDON·NEW YORK·AMSTERDAM
SYDNEY·HAMBURG·PARIS·STOCKHOLM

Original hardcover edition published in 1980
by Mills & Boon Limited

ISBN 0-373-02351-0

Harlequin edition published August 1980

Printed in U.S.A.

CHAPTER ONE

MARION did not notice the noise at first.

It must have been there in the background for some time, but it did not intrude. Any more than the small, furry honey-bees intruded, as they searched the heather for an early blossom, surprised into unexpected colour by the late June sunshine.

She sketched, intent on catching a life-likeness of a clump of breeze-dipped harebells, delicate blue against the grey rock that sheltered her from the same breeze. It was cool on the high fell top, in spite of the sunshine, and she fingered strands of hair out of her eyes, glad of the thickness of her high-necked brown sweater, which teamed with her chocolate slacks and nearly matched the colour of her eyes.

She pushed the brown velvet Alice band further back on her head. It had slipped forward, and allowed the breeze to play with the shiny honey-gold mane of hair that fell in a thick, clubbed bob almost to her shoulders. It got in her way, floating between her eyes and the harebells, and she thrust her pencil under the bulldog clip that held her sketching sheets to their stiff board backing and put down her work with a resigned sigh.

Now her concentration was slackened, the noise impinged on her consciousness. It was louder now, and harsher. Her fingers paused in their task of tucking stray gold strands back under their confining band, and she looked up, screwing up her eyes against the bright sunlight. The noise seemed to come from above her. She searched the sky, dappled with white puffballs of cloud that trailed shadows like bridal trains across the high fellside, but posed no threat to the sun, for they floated too high to bring rain.

'It's a helicopter.' She identified the small dark speck in the distance with some surprise. It probably came from the airport about fifteen miles away, on the other side of Dale End, the market town that served the valleys locally. Sometimes the fliers based there carried out exercises over the distant coastline, but it was unusual to see one this far out over the fells.

She retrieved her sketching block and pencil, and forgot the helicopter. With her hair neatly drawn back out of her eyes and into the confines of the Alice band, she recommenced her work, and became so absorbed that the sound receded again out of her consciousness. So still she remained, except for the smooth flow of her pencil across the paper, that she might have been carved from the rock against which she leaned, and a young mountain hare, oblivious of her presence, nibbled undisturbed at the heather shoots only a few feet away. Her observant eyes caught its movement, and she abandoned her work for a moment to watch it. It had on its full summer coat, and looked sleek and well fed, and she surreptitiously started to sketch again. It would make an ideal addition to the woodcut she had been commissioned to work on for a new school being built in the North.

The hare nibbled on, unconscious that its actions were about to be preserved for posterity. And then, suddenly, it stopped feeding and froze into alert watchfulness. Instantly Marion stopped sketching. Had her movements disturbed it? She was downwind of the animal, so that it could not have caught her scent. Or perhaps it was the noise of the helicopter that had frightened it? The machine was much closer to them now, drifting low over the hilltop, and coming in their direction. Its shadow, black and grotesque, moved ahead of it, flung by the sun from behind the machine, so that it ran rapidly, thrusting dark fingers across the heather-clad slope, preceding the helicopter itself.

Marion gave a grimace of disappointment. The wild creature made an ideal study, and a welcome addition to the animal frieze that was to grace the chapel of the new school, and any moment now it would bolt, and it might be weeks before she would have such an opportunity again. She remained still, wondering if it would come past her. In the manner of its kind, it would probably run uphill.

To her surprise it remained where it was. Instead of running, it suddenly clapped flat to the ground, as if someone had let all the air out of it. The black-tipped ears lay flat against its back, and only the starting eyes gave it life. Unless she had known where it was, Marion believed she would not have been able to pick it out, so well did it blend with its surroundings.

She frowned, puzzled by its unexpected behaviour. The helicopter was very close now, the noise from it a harsh, insistent rattle. It reminded Marion curiously of the warning of a rattlesnake she had heard once while she was making a research journey into the Arizona desert. She could see the heather flatten under the fierce down draught from the rotor blades, and the shadow that preceded the machine was almost on them. Unconsciously she included the hare with herself.

For some reason she shivered as she watched the moving patch of darkness claw its way across the ground towards them—and realised, suddenly, that it was the shadow, and not the noise, that had frightened the hare. The primeval fear of a shadow from above—the shadow of an eagle —had clapped the little animal to the ground in frozen immobility, and sent a momentary thrill of sympathetic fear through her own veins. It shuddered through her uncontrolled, making mockery of inherited centuries of civilisation, and brought a surge of anger in its train. Unreasonable anger, combined with reaction to being frightened, and resentment of the intruder on her peaceful afternoon.

She jumped to her feet impulsively as the helicopter rattled by overhead. It jinked upwards, as if her unexpected appearance from behind the rock caught the pilot by surprise. She gasped as the down draught caught her, and whipped her slacks legs flat against her body, streaming her hair back from her face, and she gazed upwards in mute protest. The machine carried on for a short distance, then circled and came back towards her, as if the pilot was not quite sure whether he had seen her or not, and wanted a second look. The machine was similar to the helicopters she had seen used on the television newsreels, as overhead observation posts. The cabin was little more than a transparent plastic bubble, which gave the occupants a perfect view all round them.

She thought the pilot raised his hand and waved to her, but she could not be sure. The man sitting beside him did not move. He remained still, looking down, and Marion's eyes registered a dark head and a lean, aquiline face, the features distorted slightly by the angle at which she was looking up at them, and the shape of the enclosing cabin, so that it emphasised the broad brow and the strong nose and chin and piercing eyes. She shivered again. The hovering machine, and the man's intent regard, reminded her of the fierce, hooked mask of a bird of prey.

A scuffle sounded in the heather, and a small form bounded away past her feet. The shadow had passed, it now lay well to the other side of them, and the hare grabbed its chance and bolted. The fact registered on the background of Marion's mind, while her eyes remained transfixed, held against her will by the compelling regard of the passenger in the helicopter. He moved, then. She saw his hand gesture upwards, although his lips did not seem to move, and obedient to his signal the pilot took his machine up again.

'Now he's had a look, perhaps he's satisfied,' Marion muttered to herself angrily. 'Oh!' she exclaimed furiously, as the helicopter rose, and the effect of its ascent was worse, if anything, than the down draught before. A mighty suction drew everything moveable within yards with it. A film of dust from the dry ground underneath her feet rose in a gritty cloud around her. Her clothes were too tightly fitting to rise too. She knew a moment of utter thankfulness that she was wearing slacks, and not a loose skirt.

Then her hair flowed upwards in a honey-gold stream. It was too much for the Alice band. She grabbed at it, but it eluded her fingers, and with an exclamation of annoyance she watched the velvet strip float away from her across the hillside.

Her annoyance turned to fury as a tearing sound from the block of sketching sheets on the ground warned her all was not well. The top sheet, the one that carried the results of two hours' hard work, tore away from the bulldog clip with the force of the suction drawing the paper upwards, and that, too, floated after the Alice band. She made a frantic effort to retrieve it as it passed overhead. The tip of her fingers actually touched one corner of the page before it whirled out of her reach in the wake of the helicopter.

'Bother!'

She gave a stamp of exasperation and trod on her sketching pencil, snapping it in two. She stared at it for a moment in sheer disbelief. It was a new one, and the difficulty of getting into Dale End to buy another would daunt the hardiest. Her own way of life until she came to the valley almost a year ago had been too nomadic to make owning a car worthwhile, and the bus service from Fallbeck was non-existent. The Post Office van that came to the village twice daily, morning and evening, was the only public transport available to its few inhabitants. That meant travelling out to Dale End first thing in the morning, and not being able to get back until after five o'clock. A whole day wasted, and all for the sake of one pencil. She had others, but only the one 'B' left, and it was her favourite lead for casual sketching.

The helicopter circled her, anti-clockwise, getting its bearings again, and she raised an angry face in its direction.

'Go away!' she shouted at it crossly.

Was it the glint of the sun on the cabin glass, or did a grin whip across the dark-haired passenger's face? It goaded her to fury, and she raised her fist and shook it at the intruder.

'Go away!' she shouted again, at the man this time, not the helicopter, and grabbing up her sketchblock and the remains of her smashed pencil, she spun on her heel away from her rocky shelter and hurried downhill. She wanted to run. Running would have helped her mood, but pride would not allow her to. Whatever she did, her slightest movement or gesture would be exposed to the merciless gaze of the man above her. She resisted an almost overpowering impulse to look over her shoulder, to see if he was still hovering there, still watching. . . . She knew, now, how the hare must have felt, thinking itself observed by a predator. She felt exposed and vulnerable. She would not add 'frightened' even to herself. Though why did her heart beat so fast, when she was hurrying downhill, and not climbing up?

She stumbled on, heedless of which direction she was taking, her one desire to put as much distance between herself and the helicopter as possible. She could feel the passenger's eyes following her, boring into her back. Automatically her feet found the sheep-tracks, seeking out the easier way. Her toe touched a loose piece of rock and sent it clattering downhill, and a ewe and her twin lambs erupted from behind a whin bush and scuttled away. Marion's heart raced with sudden fright, and she checked herself sharply. She was behaving like a panic-stricken refugee. Deliberately she forced herself to stop and look behind her. The helicopter was still there, hovering in roughly the same spot, but it had its tail turned towards her now, the transparent bubble of the cabin like a huge, fishy eye, was turned the other way—away from her. She felt herself go weak with relief.

'Coward!' she derided herself scornfully. But she had no control over the surge of relief that swept over her, and she resumed her journey downhill at a more normal pace, picking her way carefully now, with an eye on which end of the valley she would eventually come out at. The waters of the beck glinted below her, flowing a deep, twisted course through the rocky fields, and she chose her route with a more discriminating eye, unwilling to descend too far away from home.

She paused to survey her surroundings. She was a lot further away from the village than she had bargained for. Her headlong flight away from the high tops had brought her on a diagonal line downhill, and instead of the expected huddle of grey stone cottages round the familiar, square-towered church, the only buildings that broke the empty landscape were the house and barns of a farm, except for the windows indistinguishable at this distance from each other.

'Wade's farm,' she murmured vexedly. She did not think she had come so far out of her way. And she did not particularly want to cross the Wades' land if she could help it. She knew the family slightly. She usually tried to avoid Zilla Wade if she could, but it was difficult when the village only boasted the one shop-cum-Post Office, and the proprietress looked upon each of her customers as a heaven-sent opportunity for a gossip, which the sharp-tongued, middle-aged farmer's wife was never reluctant to indulge in.

Aaron Wade was as surly as his wife was shrill, and the son seemed to Marion to be an unprepossessing mixture of the two. She had seen both the men in the Fleece from time to time. It looked like Benjamin Wade in the field immediately below her now. She could see a black-haired youth with a cringing dog at his heels, shutting a gate on a small flock of bleating sheep that looked as if they might have come from a high-sided lorry parked nearby.

She turned away, taking another sheep-track that she hoped would bring her down further along the beck and so miss the farmer's son, but his dog must have noticed her movement because it looked up and challenged her, and she frowned as its master, too, turned and saw her.

'Oh well....' She shrugged and continued on her way. 'Ben can only be unpleasant if I'm trespassing. Thank goodness it's the son, and not the father.'

'I was watching the helicopter, and missed the path down,' she called out as she neared him. Attack seemed to be her best form of defence, and she spoke first. Ben remained where he was, obviously waiting for her to descend, and to her chagrin the sheep-track she followed turned sharply down towards him, giving her no choice of route unless she picked her way across a patch of bog. Ben was better than getting her feet wet, she decided, and she greeted him with forced cheerfulness. 'I wonder what they've come across this way for? I thought they usually carried out their exercises over the coast,' she indicated the helicopter still hovering over the tops.

'Looking for lost hikers, as like as not.' At least Ben did not seem disposed to be unpleasant, she thought thankfully. She supposed in his rough, gypsy fashion he might even be attractive, if he tidied himself up. Not that he had got much incentive in this isolated spot, she thought with a flash of sympathy for the youth. She imagined him to be about twenty-two, roughly three years younger than she was herself, and already he seemed to be developing his father's surly nature, which the enforced loneliness of his home life would do nothing to help. There was little enough for young people to do in Fallbeck, and it was a long journey into Dale End.

'We'll all have to keep a lookout,' she suggested, and Ben's face darkened into a scowl.

'I've got suthin' better to do'n go searching for lost hikers,' he growled. 'Though from the looks of it, they might have found what they came looking for, anyway.' He jerked his head upwards, and Marion followed his gaze.

'I didn't see anybody on the other slope while I was on the tops,' she commented in a puzzled voice.

The helicopter still hovered, but now a dark blob appeared out of its belly. It straightened out into the form of a man, and faintly Marion could see the thin line of a rope of some kind from which he appeared to be suspended.

'I wish I'd stayed on top and watched.' She began to regret her impulsive departure. The descending figure disappeared out of sight as it neared the ground, and after what seemed a long wait it reappeared again over the edge of the ridge, hanging like a spider on the end of a web. Some mechanism inside the machine drew its burden upwards, and the man disappeared inside.

'It couldn't have been a hiker,' Ben commented, 'he'd got no one else with him going back up.'

'Perhaps he's just practising,' Marion suggested vaguely, and the youth gave a scornful snort.

'Pity some folks haven't got anything better to do.' He snapped impatient fingers at his dog, and without a backwards glance he slouched off towards the lorry, and left Marion standing where she was.

'Isolation doesn't help his manners, either,' she decided, sharply critical. She did not expect Ben to offer her a lift into Fallbeck, the Wades were not known locally for their generosity. 'Close,' Mrs Pugh called them. But at least he could have bade her a civil goodbye.

She thrust the unwelcome encounter out of her mind with a shrug. It was part and parcel of a spoiled afternoon. What with the helicopter, and losing her drawing, to say nothing of her hairband, it had been a wasted journey to the fell. If the weather remained fine she would try to get back to make another sketch of the clump of harebells, before the end of the week. She wanted the harebells for a corner of the woodcut. She glanced up at the sky. It looked settled enough. It was high, and blue, with only a few small white clouds floating across it. And the dark speck of the helicopter, still there as well. Marion frowned.

'I thought the wretched thing had gone away,' she muttered, irritated by its persistence. It seemed to be coming along her own route, following the line of the beck—almost, she thought crossly, as if it was following her. She quickened her steps, but by the time she gained the village street it was still there. Fallbeck possessed only one street, the paved road came to an end at the entrance to the Wades' holding, the bleak rise of Fallbeck Scar just beyond, bisected by the white ribbon of a waterfall that gave birth to the beck, effectively blocked off the valley at one end, so that the road makers found it easier to take their highway through Merevale, a shallower and more gently contoured valley on the other side of the watershed, which did not offer the competition of a river.

'Look, Miss Dorman! It's a whirlybird!'

A group of children called out to her from where they clustered round the gate of their school, too interested in the unusual appearance of the helicopter to bother that it was home time. Marion smiled at their elderly tutor. The dozen children were his entire school, but despite the isolation of their valley they had all the modern television jargon off pat, she thought with amusement.

'I wonder what they're doing over here?' John Cornish spoke pleasantly, as interested as his pupils.

'Ben Wade seemed to think it might be a lost hiker,' Marion joined the group looking up.

'I think we'd have heard, if it was. The police always used to get in touch if there was anyone missing on the fells.'

'I don't remember any searches being carried out since I've been back at the Fleece,' Marion answered.

'We don't get many walkers hereabouts now, not since the bus service was discontinued,' the schoolmaster said regretfully. 'That must be over two years ago, long before you came to stay with your uncle.'

'Perhaps they're thinking of starting a helicopter service instead,' Marion suggested with a mischievous look towards the children.

'I doubt it, but you've certainly started something,' John Cornish laughed at the instant clamour that arose from round him. 'Miss Dorman was only joking,' he stilled it into disappointed groans. 'But if there's anything of the kind going on, I expect the children will hear about it long before we do,' he predicted ruefully.

'Pass on the news when you get it,' Marion begged,

smiling. 'I mustn't stay here and watch any longer, I promised to help Mrs Pugh with the dinner.' She did not want to remain and watch the helicopter. Her nerves still prickled from their encounter on the hilltop, and she turned across the street, thankful that she was within yards of the shelter of home. She actually stood on the step of the Fleece, with her hand on the door knob, when a shriek from the children spun her round and riveted her attention first on them, and then on the sky again. She followed their excitedly pointing fingers.

'He's coming down, look! He's landing!'

He was not, but he was very low, she thought, frowning. The harsh rattle of the rotor blades seemed to fill the village street. It bounced back from the stone-walled cottages, the echo intensifying the noise into what, to Marion's heightened sensitivity, seemed to be of deafening proportions. Instinctively she raised her hands to her ears, forgetting she still carried her sketchbook. The corner of it caught her sharply on her cheek, and she let it go. She grabbed at it hastily and missed, and it slid to the step with a clatter.

'For goodness' sake!' Would the machine and its dreadful occupants haunt her for the rest of the day? she wondered furiously. She raised angry eyes towards it as it hovered at little more than roof height, cruising slowly towards her along the length of the village street, and her breath caught in her throat as, for the second time that afternoon, she met the piercing regard of the man sitting next to the pilot. It lanced downwards and seemed to spear right through her, rooting her to the spot. She felt like the hare, exposed, and defenceless. She shivered, and the movement brought her to life. Unlike the hare, she had a refuge to run to.

In a blind panic, of which she was to feel ashamed minutes later, she wrenched at the knob in her hand and flung the door open with a resounding crash, which met the echo of a second bang as she fled inside and slammed the door behind her.

CHAPTER TWO

'WHATEVER'S going on?'

Marion pulled herself off the door as Mrs Pugh's voice came from along the stone flagged corridor leading from the kitchen.

'It's only me. I let the door go, and it slammed,' she called back, her moment of weakness past. For a brief second, until she gained the shelter of the house, black terror possessed her, and she leaned against the closed door, using it as a prop to steady her shaking limbs. Shame possessed her now, in a hot flood. It lent colour to her cheeks that had been chalk-white a moment before, and she turned to her uncle's housekeeper with her confidence more or less restored.

'I pushed the door to a bit hard to shut out the noise of the helicopter,' she said, as if shutting out the noise of helicopters was an everyday occurrence. Mrs Pugh's attractive blue eyes were windows for a shrewd mind, and Marion did not feel up to the task of explaining irrational fears that she could not explain even to herself.

'What's a helicopter doing over Fallbeck, I wonder?' Mrs Pugh craned her head at the nearest window. 'He's going away now, whatever he came for.' The receding noise already told Marion that, but hearing the house-keeper's calm voice confirm it helped to restore her poise to normal.

'Ben Wade seemed to think it might be a lost hiker. I met him on the way down the fell,' Marion explained. She did not mention her encounter with the helicopter on the fell top. For some reason she felt reluctant to discuss it, even with Mrs Pugh.

'Did you get the sketch you wanted while you were up there?' The comfortably rounded housekeeper deserted her post at the window as the noise of the aircraft dwindled into silence. 'I thought you took your sketchblock out with you?' Affection made the grey-haired little woman observant.

'I did. I left it on the step, I was in such a hurry to shut out the rattle of that beastly machine,' Marion said confusedly. She had forgotten her sketchblock was still on the step outside, where she dropped it. 'I'll go and pick it up.' She opened the door hurriedly before the housekeeper could question her further, and hoped fervently she would not be asked to show the results of her afternoon's work. Mrs Pugh took a keen interest in her work, and normally Marion welcomed the opportunity to talk about it. But not today. She found she did not want to talk about today, to anyone.

'I'll take it upstairs and dust it off.' She retrieved her ill-used sketchblock and the two ends of the snapped pencil, and made a pretence of rubbing her sleeve across the top page.

'Has it spoiled your sketch?' The housekeeper clicked her tongue sympathetically. 'Let me see ... oh, drat that phone!' she exclaimed as a loud summons issued from the other end of the passage. 'I'd better go and see who it is. It rang earlier on, just when I'd got my hands all flour from the baking, and your uncle, he was that deep in his books he didn't hear it. By the time I got to the hall it had stopped.'

'And you've been wondering who it was ever since?' guessed Marion with a chuckle. She took advantage of the interruption and slipped upstairs, and tossed her sketching materials into her bedroom cupboard, safely out of the way.

'Well, I know now,' the housekeeper returned triumphantly, just as Marion came downstairs again. 'They said they'd rung us earlier and there'd been no answer, and we haven't had any other calls today.'

That was not unusual, thought Marion with a prick of worry. John Cornish had been correct when he said the discontinued bus service had affected the number of walkers who came to the valley. Fallbeck Scar offered an attractive rock climb, and at weekends the Fleece used to be fully booked with sports enthusiasts, but since she returned a year ago the hotel had only entertained an occasional visitor. Lack of public transport made the walkers seek more easily accessible country, and the trade at the hotel, and the one village shop, suffered accordingly.

The Fleece paid its way, but only just, but nowadays it did not seem to worry her uncle unduly. The pucker in Marion's forehead deepened. Since her aunt died, Miles Dorman had retreated more and more into his world of books, and so long as the hotel made an adequate return he did not seem to care greatly.

'Things are looking up.' Marion smiled at the sparkle in the older woman's eyes.

'It's about time,' Mrs Pugh declared forthrightly. 'Things have been over-quiet for too long. We'll be getting slack if we're not careful.'

'There's no chance of that.' The plump little housekeeper kept standards that would do justice to a much bigger establishment, but Marion knew she liked a bit more 'stir' round her, as she called it. She would enjoy having visitors, no matter how long they decided to stay.

'I'll go and prepare a room for them,' she offered.

'Two rooms. Single ones, plus bath, both in the name of a Mr Harland,' Mrs Pugh corrected her. 'Make sure you use the best towels out of the top shelf of the linen cupboard, they'll go with the curtains in the single rooms along the corridor from yours.'

'Mr Harland and his companion will have every comfort,' Marion promised. 'I'll make the rooms look nice, they sound as if they might be an engaged couple,' she hazarded.

'The person on the phone didn't say, but it was a woman who booked the rooms,' the housekeeper agreed with her reasoning.

'That settles it.' Marion went about her task happily.

It would be pleasant to have company of her own age in the hotel. In Fallbeck itself, for that matter. Most of the small population was either middle-aged or elderly, or young children. Ben Wade was about the nearest person to her own age left in the valley, and given such a choice, Marion preferred her own company.

'I'm looking forward to meeting them,' she decided, and on an impulse she ran downstairs to pick a handful of old-fashioned cream tea roses that made a perfumed glory of the garden wall outside. 'I'll put the girl in the room at the head of the stairs,' she called through to Mrs Pugh. 'It's next to mine, and it's the larger of the two single ones.'

The effect was both comfortable and welcoming, she thought with a last satisfied look at the results of her efforts. Both rooms were alike, with plain, modern furniture which had the dual advantage of twentieth-century comfort without clashing with the old, beamed rooms. Plain brown carpets set off gold curtains and covers, and white-emulsioned walls which age made too uneven for wallpaper to be practical. A brown pottery jug of tea roses added just the right personal touch, she decided, to make the occupant of the larger room feel extra welcome. Marion glanced at her watch. She had been longer than she intended, but she felt the results justified her efforts, and hoped they would be appreciated. If their guests intended arriving for dinner, they should be here at any minute.

'Will you answer the door, please, Marion? I'm just in the middle of making the gravy.'

The old-fashioned spring doorbell clanged a warning, Mrs Pugh called out simultaneously from the kitchen, and Marion hurried downstairs. Briefly she wished she had time to change out of her slacks and sweater, but it was too late now. She swung open the heavy studded door with a welcoming smile.

'Come in. You're just in time for dinner.'

'Good evening. I'm Reeve Harland. This is. . . .'

Out of a daze of shock she caught the name 'Willy', but the rest escaped her. She felt her hand grasped and shaken, and the welcoming smile faded from her face as she stared in stunned disbelief straight into the dark, hawk visage of the passenger in the helicopter.

'His eyes are grey.' Through the haze the clear, cool colour registered on her consciousness. They were the grey of a mountain lake. Warm grey under the smile of the summer sun. Steely grey and hard under the dark storms of winter. . . .

'We've booked two rooms. This is the Fleece, isn't it?' The man called Willy recalled her to her senses. With an effort she pulled her eyes away from the dark face above her and released her hand at the same time. Her cheeks went hot as she realised she had left it in the stranger's grasp for what must seem an unconscionable time to him. She glanced up at him quickly, and her confusion deepened as she caught an amused light in the grey eyes, which it seemed had never left her face.

'Er—yes—of course. You spoke to Mrs Pugh.' She stammered to a halt. He had not; the housekeeper said it was a woman who made the booking. She took a deep breath and tried again. 'Come upstairs and see your rooms. Dinner will be in about twenty minutes.' That would give her time to gather her wits, she thought desperately, and wished with all her heart she had not offered to serve the guests herself, to save Mrs Pugh the trouble. She turned her back on them and hastened towards the stairs. And knew without looking back that it was Reeve Harland, and not his companion, who came soft-footed behind her. She could feel his look boring into her back, just as she had felt it on the hillside.

'Both the rooms are alike,' she spoke breathlessly, and hoped the man following her would think it was her hurried ascent of the stairs that was to blame. 'The room at the head of the stairs is the larger of the two.'

'I'll take the other one, then,' the man called Willy decided. 'Heights make me dizzy,' he said solemnly, and grinned suddenly at Marion's startled look.

'But you're the helicopter pilot,' she began, and stopped

herself furiously. She had not meant to betray the fact that she recognised them. Now it was out, and she could not undo it. She bit her lip vexedly. Willy's joking was merely his manner of making way gracefully for the other, obviously more senior man, to take the larger room. She remembered belatedly that the accommodation had been booked in Reeve Harland's name.

'Ah, but when I'm driving the 'copter I don't have time to look down. I leave that to my passenger,' he said significantly.

'Cut along and get ready for dinner,' Reeve Harland interrupted him. 'We don't want to be late for our first meal here.'

How long did they intend to remain? wondered Marion uneasily, and yearned for the days when the valley boasted a bus service, and during the summer months they often had to turn away prospective guests because they were already full. There was no chance of using pre-booked rooms as an excuse to get rid of these two quickly.

'This is my room, I take it?' Reeve Harland's hand was on the door knob, opening the door, and there was the hint of impatience in his manner.

'Yes—oh!' Marion's hand rose to her mouth uncertainly. 'But I put a bowl of roses in there. I thought. . . .' How could she tell this tall, slim stranger who towered above her that she thought he would be a girl? Her courage failed her, and she stopped speaking.

'I'm very fond of roses.' His cool gaze held hers for a long second, then with a nod he stepped inside the room. The room next to her own. She resisted the impulse to dive inside her bedroom out of sight. The thought of Reeve Harland next door took away its sanctuary. She heard his case thump on the trestle put at the bottom of the bed for that purpose, and the sound broke the spell that seemed to freeze her feet to the floor. She turned and fled downstairs, and sought refuge in the kitchen with Mrs Pugh.

'He's not a girl. I mean, he's two men. I mean. . . .'

'What do you mean?' Mrs Pugh sent her a straight look over the bowl of gravy. 'What's the matter with you? You've not seemed yourself since you came back from the fell this afternoon,' she observed shrewdly. 'Has that Ben Wade been bothering you?' Her tone sharpened.

'Ben Wade? Good heavens, no!' Marion's surprised look was so obviously genuine that the housekeeper's face cleared.

'That's all right, then,' she said in a relieved tone of voice, and put the gravy aside. 'If you've nothing else to do, you can go and lay the table in the dining room for me.'

'I can see to the rest of the dinner in here for you, if you like.' Marion did not want to meet their guests again if she could help it.

'There's no need,' Mrs Pugh denied her. 'Just lay the table, then you can run upstairs and get changed yourself.'

And risk meeting Reeve Harland on his way down, thought Marion. The possibility put speed into her actions. If she hurried, she might be in time to miss him. She shook snowy linen across the end of the long, dark oak refectory table, and after a brief hesitation she laid two places opposite to one another, ignoring the seat at the head of the table. She felt sure if she set a place there, Reeve would automatically take it as his right, and an obscure resentment made her determined he should not have the opportunity.

'You gave me a fright, this afternoon!'

She spun round and dropped a handful of cutlery with a clatter, as a male voice spoke from just behind her.

'Sorry!' it apologised. 'Now I've given you one.' Willy smiled at her ruefully. 'I didn't mean to play tit for tat, honestly.' His round face beamed in a friendly fashion, and Marion could not help smiling back. She liked the pilot, she decided. He reminded her of a cheerful egg. He was short and round, and almost bald, with merry blue eyes and an engaging smile. The antithesis of his friend—

colleague—boss—whatever Reeve Harland was to him. 'Here, let me pick it up for you, it's gone under the side-board somewhere.' With surprising agility the corpulent little pilot retrieved the errant teaspoon and handed it back into Marion's nerveless fingers.

'*I* frightened *you*?' She found her voice. What did he think his appearance with the helicopter had done to her nerves? she wondered. But it was difficult, she discovered, to feel cross with Willy.

'We were cruising a bit low across the fells,' he admitted, 'but I didn't expect anyone to jump up from behind a rock like that. I thought there'd be nothing but sheep up there, and then you popped up like a jack-in-the-box.' He grinned suddenly. 'I must admit you made a pleasant change from sheep. But your sudden appearance like that shook the Skipper too. He insisted on us coming back to see if you were O.K., in case we'd upset you or anything.'

So Reeve Harland had insisted, had he? she thought tartly. She could well have done without the dark-haired man's concern.

'I don't upset so easily,' she said offhandedly, 'but I thought I saw you wave to me when you crossed the fell top,' she prevaricated. She did not want to discuss Reeve Harland, particularly with Willy.

'You saw right,' he nodded agreeably, 'but you didn't wave back,' he accused her. 'But then girls never do wave back. At least, not to me,' he said mournfully.

No doubt they would have waved back to Reeve. He probably took it for granted that they did.

'I saw you shake your fist at us, though,' Willy shot her an enquiring glance, and ejected her out of her momentary calm. She nearly dropped the cutlery again.

'Oh, that. . . .' She tightened her grip on the spoons convulsively. She had forgotten her impulsive gesture. She had not thought she would see either the pilot or his passenger again, let alone have them lodging with her in the same house, and she bitterly regretted giving way to the childish retaliation.

'We did give you a fright after all.' Willy eyed her keenly. 'You looked real mad,' he remembered.

'I was mad.' Marion forced a laugh. 'The down draught from your rotors caught me by surprise, and I stepped back and trod on my sketching pencil. Just for the minute, I could have cheerfully stood on you, too,' she confessed with a shamefaced grin. She found she could laugh about the incident now, with Willy.

'I can't say I blame you,' he returned sympathetically. 'I should have felt the same. You must add it on to Reeve's account for the rooms,' he advised her, and unwittingly recalled her to the original reason for her haste.

'He won't be inclined to pay his bill at all if he's kept waiting for meals.' Marion hurriedly set out the rest of the cutlery. 'Dinner's almost ready, and I'm not changed yet.' The open friendliness of the middle-aged pilot had tempted her to stay talking for longer than she should.

'The evening papers have just come.' She handed them over. 'They'll while away the time for you until your friend comes down.' She obliquely laid the blame for delaying the meal on their other guest. Mrs Pugh would not serve the soup until they were both in the dining room. Marion left Willy reading and hastened towards the stairs. She was half way up them when Reeve Harland's door opened. If she had been nearer to the bottom she would have retreated, pretending she had forgotten something, but positioned as she was in the middle of the flight, it would look too obvious. She hesitated, but only for a moment. Her chin rose defiantly, and she continued upwards, acutely conscious of the tall, dark-haired figure standing at the head of the stairs, watching her ascent.

'I wish he wouldn't look at me like that,' she said to herself forcefully. She simmered with silent resentment. If he had got any manners at all, he would look the other way. Marion's complete lack of self-consciousness so far as her own looks were concerned made her unaware that her unusual colouring, perfect skin and lissom figure were sufficient to draw the eyes of any stranger, particularly a

man. The grey ones watching her kindled with apprecia-
tion, but they were veiled again by the time she reached
the landing, and spoke to him breathlessly.

'Dinner's ready as soon as you go down. Willy's already
in the dining room.'

'Willy, eh?' He spoke, then, and the veil lifted on sudden
laughter. Marion's colour rose treacherously.

'I didn't catch his other name,' she began defensively.
Did this creature think she called any man by his Christian
name after five minutes' acquaintance? she wondered
hotly.

'Willy will do nicely,' he told her gravely. 'If you call
him anything else he'll wonder who you're talking to.' The
laughter reached his voice as he turned away, and Marion
glared at his retreating back as he ran lightly downstairs.
The steel grey jacket of his lounge suit fitted his broad
shoulders like a glove, the sombre colour making him look
taller and slimmer, if anything, than he really was. A
maroon and grey striped silk tie added a discreet touch of
colour against an ivory silk shirt and—she gasped at his
impudence—he wore a small cream rosebud in the lapel
of his jacket. One of the tea roses she had put in the vase
in his room.

Did he hear the sound of her indrawn breath? If not,
what else made him turn as he reached the bottom of the
stairs, and look up, directly at her? And discover her still
on the landing, watching him. For a long endless
minute grey eyes met brown ones. His look speared upwards like a shaft of light in the cool dimness of the stairway. And then Mrs Pugh struck the gong and he turned
away, and Marion felt as if shackles had dropped from her
feet, releasing her. She spun round and ran to her bedroom door, grasped the knob and threw it open, as she
had thrown open the front door of the hotel only that
afternoon, and ran inside, slamming it behind her. She did
not care if he heard it slam, she could not help it, and
coherent thought was beyond her. She sank down on to
her bed, feeling herself begin to tremble.

'Marion, are you coming down? Your dinner will be cold.'

How long she sat there she did not know. Mrs Pugh's call sounded as if she might be coming upstairs in search of her, and urgency moved Marion on to her feet. She called back,

'I'm coming. I didn't realise I'd been so long.'

Her voice must have sounded normal enough, because the housekeeper's footsteps went off back downstairs, and Marion stripped off her sweater with hasty hands. It would not do for Mrs Pugh to come back and find she had not even started to change. She plucked a dress at random from her wardrobe. It was a high-necked, sleeveless leaf green linen, a perfect foil for her honey-gold hair. She subdued the latter into a smooth curtain with a hasty brush, slipped on a pair of white sandals, and ran downstairs before the older woman waxed impatient.

'Sorry I was so long.' Conscience reminded her she had offered to serve the guests' dinner herself, but Mrs Pugh did not seem put out by her delinquency.

'Don't worry about Mr Harland and his pilot,' she said comfortably, 'they're settled with their main course.'

Marion was not worried about them. Her last concern was for Reeve Harland's comfort, though it should be her first, she thought guiltily, since he was staying in her uncle's hotel.

'They seem a pleasant pair,' the housekeeper went on happily. 'They tell me they've parked their helicopter at the airport.'

'And parked themselves on us,' Marion observed sourly, if somewhat obscurely through a mouthful of crisp Yorkshire pudding.

'Well, that's what we're here for, isn't it?' Mercifully Mrs Pugh did not seem to notice the ire in her voice, and she pulled herself up sharply. If she made her dislike of Reeve Harland too obvious, the housekeeper might want to know why, and Marion found it difficult enough to discover a rational explanation, even to herself. 'We're just not on the same wavelength,' she dismissed their dark-haired guest with a shrug, and concentrated on her meal.

'I'll take the sweet in.' Mrs Pugh cut generous portions of apple pie. 'You can look after their coffee while I give your uncle his meal.'

'Has the man come to look after the bar?' Someone would have to be on duty, it was past opening time, and she added hastily as she caught the housekeeper's look of surprise, 'I know I don't normally serve in there, I just hadn't heard Jim arrive, that's all.'

'He came while you were busy upstairs. I hope they like apple pie,' her companion returned to more immediate concerns.

'I'm sure Willy does,' Marion smiled. And Reeve Harland could either eat it or go without, she added silently to herself.

'I've told them you'll take their coffee into the drawing room in a quarter of an hour.' Mrs Pugh returned as Marion finished her own meal. 'Now I'll go and try to part your uncle from his encyclopaedias for long enough to eat his dinner,' she said without much hope in her voice.

'You go ahead, I'll clear the table in the dining room.' Conscience made Marion offer. If she put the coffee tray in the drawing room a few minutes before Reeve and Willy were ready to go in, as soon as they were safely installed she could return and clear the dining room table, and she need not come face to face with either of them.

The first half of her plan worked nicely. She had just deposited the coffee tray when her straining ears caught the sounds of exodus from the dining room. She slipped hurriedly back to the kitchen, thankful for once for the twist in the passage which hid her from sight, and as soon as the drawing room door closed she slipped out again with an empty tray in her hands, to clear the dinner table. The first intimation she had that the second half of her plan had gone awry was when Reeve spoke from behind her.

'I believe these are your property.'

It was a good job the tray of crockery was rested on the table, otherwise it would have gone the way of the cutlery earlier, with disastrous results. He must have returned to the dining room almost immediately. Perhaps he had forgotten something, maybe the evening papers. Willy had left them on one of the chairs. She drew a deep breath, and turned reluctantly to face him.

'Your sketching is very good.' Was he being condescending? Marion eyed him suspiciously, but he went on smoothly, 'Did we disturb the hare, as well as the artist?' So he recognised her drawing for what it was. He held it out to her, loosely rolled, and bound with something soft and brown. Her hair ribbon.

'How did you...?' Marion ignored his question and asked one of her own. How had he come to be in possession of her drawing and ribbon? The last time she had seen them, they were both floating downhill, pulled by the suction from the rising helicopter.

'Naturally I retrieved them for you,' Reeve told her coolly. 'Since it was our fault you lost them, it was up to us to get them back for you.'

'It was you who dropped from the helicopter?' Suddenly she remembered the machine hovering, and the dark figure descending from it. She swallowed convulsively, seeing again in her mind's eye the spider-thin thread by which he had hung. 'What a risk to take, for the sake of a sheet of paper, and a strip of velvet ribbon!' The words came out before she could stop them, but she could not help it. She shivered at the thought that anyone would go to such lengths for such a trivial reason.

'There was no risk.' He spoke with calm self-assurance, and Marion felt a mounting irritation with the man. His quixotic action had put her at a disadvantage, and what was worse, she was now under an obligation to him, and the feeling rankled. 'Though perhaps I should have left the velvet ribbon on the hill,' he eyed her speculatively, 'it seems a shame to confine such lovely hair.'

'It gets in my eyes when I'm sketching.' Marion coloured furiously. How dared he criticise her mode of dress!

'If you'd waited a little longer on the hilltop, you could have had it back right away.'

'There wasn't time—I had to get home, and it's a long walk.'

'Yes, we saw you go.' Saw her run away, like the frightened hare? Marion gritted her teeth and remained silent. 'Diana, striding the uplands,' he murmured, and her eyes sparked angrily.

'My name's Marion,' she snapped, and realised too late that she had given him just the information he wanted.

'Oh, you've cleared the table.' Mrs Pugh broke the tension, that felt to Marion as if it might snap with an audible crack. 'Of course,' the housekeeper clicked her tongue vexedly, 'you told me you would, I just forgot.' She bustled up to the table and the loaded tray. 'I might as well take this while I'm here, and you can fold up the cloth. Was there anything else you wanted, Mr Harland?' She looked enquiringly from Reeve to Marion, patently wondering what it was they had been talking about.

'Mr Harland returned my hairband. He found it,' Marion began. She looked straight at Reeve then, and her eyes begged him not to say where he found it, or how it came to be in his possession. There was no earthly reason why Mrs Pugh should not know, except that inexplicably Marion did not want to talk about it to anyone.

'That was nice,' the housekeeper raised the laden tray. 'I hope you've thanked him properly.' She never quite grasped the fact that Marion was no longer a leggy schoolgirl needing guidance.

'Thank you.' She faced Reeve as the door closed behind the older woman, and her stiffly formal tone expressed little gratitude. A strange light lit the grey eyes looking down at her.

'She didn't say just to thank me,' he reminded Marion softly, 'she said to thank me properly,' he emphasised.

Before she had time to realise what he was going to do

he reached out and grasped her by the shoulders and turned her towards him. She raised her face in quick protest at his touch, and instantly his lips descended on hers, claiming, without asking, the extra thanks that he thought were his due.

CHAPTER THREE

SURPRISE held her rigid for a second or two. Seconds in which a treacherous sweetness stole through her veins, electrifying her lips, and the touch of his hands on her shoulders. As if in a dream she felt herself respond, the rigidity leave her.

'No!' She wrenched herself free, felt the rosebud in his lapel brush her cheek as she twisted frantically free from his grasp, and gathering up the tablecloth in a crumpled heap in her arms, she whirled away from him and ran from the room. Willy appeared at the drawing room door as she rounded the corner of the passage.

'I wanted Reeve,' he began.

'You can have him!' choked Marion, and fled on until the kitchen door closed behind her, and she leaned against it gratefully, shaking in every limb, with the tablecloth still clutched to her as if to ward off she did not know what.

'Dearie me, that cloth'll be all crumples if you hold it like that.' Mrs Pugh came in and clicked her tongue disapprovingly.

'I was just going outside to shake it.' Marion grasped at the first excuse to enter her head.

'What for?' the housekeeper asked. 'There weren't any crumbs. They didn't eat their bread rolls.'

'I didn't notice—it won't matter then—I'll fold it.' Marion felt herself becoming incoherent, and she held the cloth high, stroking it back to smooth folds, and using it as a shield to hide her burning face. Fortunately the cloth

was a large one, and her action did not look strange, as the
length of it was as much as her arms could manage at one
stretch. Reeve had been more than her arms could manage.
His mocking laugh echoed in her head, taunting her. Why
had she responded to his kiss like that? Her cheeks flamed
at the memory. Anyone would think he was the first man
who had kissed her. She had met many men in her travels,
more than one had wanted to marry her, but with an instinctive caution Marion managed to remain unattached and
curiously heartwhole for her twenty-five years. Applying
the same philosophy which she used with Ben Wade, she
preferred to remain aloof, contenting herself with the fulfilment her work offered until she should find the greater
fulfilment which she knew life with the right man could
hold for her. And Reeve Harland was definitely not the
right man.

His stolen kiss amounted to an insult. Even the act of
retrieving her drawing and her hair ribbon from the fellside in such an unorthodox manner did not give him the
right to presume so far. The thought gave her pause. In
her desperate haste to get away from Reeve, she had left
both the drawing and the hair ribbon behind her in the
dining room. And if she went back to get them, she might
encounter Reeve again.

'I'll get them in the morning.' She did not realise she had
spoken out loud until Mrs Pugh answered her.

'Get what in the morning? There's nothing else for you
to do here, so you can get whatever it is now.'

'I won't bother,' Marion answered hastily, 'it's only my
hairband, I left it in the dining room.'

'And after Mr Harland took the trouble to return it to
you,' the housekeeper reproached her. 'Though I must say
I like your hair free myself, like you've got it now.'

Marion half hoped Mrs Pugh would offer to get the
hairband for her, but she did not seem to have any further
business in the dining room that evening, and when Marion
went to look for her property the next morning it was not
there. Neither was her drawing. She frowned, nonplussed,

and then her face cleared. Perhaps their daily help had tidied it away. She was a great one for tidying things away.

'I expect it'll be on my bed,' Marion decided with relief. That was where their daily usually put odds and ends she could not identify, and left Marion to sort out their owners. Everything from a gold bracelet to half a gumboot had found its way there during the last twelve months. But when she went up to her bedroom to get ready to go out, neither the hairband nor the drawing had arrived yet.

'I won't bother with it now,' she answered Mrs Pugh's enquiry, 'I want to catch the post van into Dale End. Is there anything you need while I'm there?'

'There's a list of books your uncle wants from the library, and there's probably some due to go back.'

'I've got both,' Marion answered her, 'that's why I particularly want to go in today or they'll be overdue. And I need some new sketching pencils for myself.' She wanted only the one, and she would not have needed that, she thought with asperity, if it had not been for Reeve and his wretched helicopter. It did not strike her as illogical that she blamed only Reeve, and not Willy as well.

'I thought I saw Mr Harland,' the housekeeper began, and Marion interrupted her hastily. She did not want to hear about Reeve Harland, his movements held no interest for her, she told herself, except that she preferred them to be in the opposite direction to her own.

'I'll have to go, or I'll miss the post van. I saw him go down towards Wade's farm about twenty minutes ago.' There was no gainsaying her excuse, if she missed the van her opportunity to go to Dale End would be irretrievably lost until the following morning. She ran down the steps and paused on the bottom one. A sleek Rover was pulled up at the side of the street, and Willy and Reeve leaned against the bonnet, deep in discussion. They saw her and straightened to their feet just as she caught sight of the post van.

'Oh, wave him to stop for me!' The driver was evidently in a hurry, and her hesitation on the hotel step lost her the necessary precious seconds to attract his attention in time to pick her up. She let out a puff of relief as Willy obligingly waved, and the van driver slowed to a halt and leaned out to speak to him—and then stared with incredulous fury as Reeve deliberately sauntered to the van shaking his head, and actually motioned the driver to carry on. Which he did, without ado. Marion ran towards him, waving frantically, but the van driver could not have seen her, for he went serenely on his way, leaving her with an armful of heavy books, stranded by the side of the road.

'What did you send him off for?' she cried furiously, turning on Reeve. 'You knew I wanted him.'

'Because we can give you a much more comfortable ride into Dale End in the car.' He did not look in the least abashed.

'How do you know I want to go into Dale End? I might want to....'

'Because that's where the post van goes to,' he interrupted her confidently. 'There isn't anywhere else he could drop you.'

What he said was perfectly true. Just as it was true that the Rover would be infinitely more comfortable to ride in than the van. The post vehicle was like most basic amenities, indispensable, but still basic.

'For a stranger to the district you seem to know a lot about our public transport facilities,' she snapped ungraciously.

'I made it my business to find out,' he answered her coolly. And as he spoke he shot a glance at the pilot. Willy began to speak. He got as far as, 'We've been looking....' Then he caught Reeve's eye, and subsided into silence.

It was almost as if Reeve's look warned the pilot of something. But what? She cast the two a puzzled glance. If they were based at the aerodrome, it seemed natural enough for them to want to explore the district while they were there, although—Marion glanced at the sleek luxury

car—they would hardly stand in need of the public transport facilities, such as they were. It struck her suddenly that
she had not seen either of the men in uniform. Perhaps
Reeve did not have to wear one, although he had about him
an air of confident authority that would fit well with rank.
But surely if they belonged to one of the airlines, Willy,
as the pilot, would be required to don the garb of his
status. They were both in mufti now, Willy in sweater and
denims, which kept his portly form tidy without trouble,
and Reeve in black, tightly fitting slacks and a white
open-necked shirt with the sleeves rolled above his elbows,
showing darkly tanned, muscular arms. Marion felt glad,
now, she had not succumbed to an earlier temptation to
dress in the slacks and sweater she wore yesterday, which
would have been ideal for a ride in the post van, but her
slender-fitting cream skirt and brown shirt-blouse pleated
to her waist by a brown patent leather belt were a more
fitting outfit for a car ride into town.

'Would you like to travel in the front or the back?'
Willy asked hopefully, and Marion hesitated. She did not
want to travel in either. Her first instinct was to refuse to
travel with them at all. But she had promised to obtain a
special book for her uncle. The library had telephoned
to say it was ready, and she did not want to disappoint
him. He was something of a historian, and in his spare
time he was writing a book on road building going back
to the earliest times, and the changes, both beneficial and
otherwise, that it had brought in its train. The book he
wanted from the library was a reference volume that would
be invaluable to him at the stage he had just reached. The
weight of the books under her arm reminded her of her
obligations to her only relative. She could feel Reeve's eyes
on her, watching to see what her reaction would be. No
doubt he would think he had won, but she knew the real
reason for accepting a lift from him, if he did not. She
shrugged with feigned indifference, and tried to ignore
the gleam her submission brought to the grey eyes.

'In front, please.' That way she would have Willy's

company in the driving seat, not Reeve's. She felt grateful that the car did not have a front bench seat that would accommodate three.

'Let me take your books, they look heavy.' Reeve held out his hands for them. 'They'll travel in the back of the car quite safely,' he insisted as she hesitated, and she relinquished them in silence. He waited for a second or two while Willy handed her into the car and shut the door, and then he went round to the other side, and Marion sat back and relaxed. She could rely on Willy, she felt sure, to keep up a cheerful flow of conversation, and with Reeve safely ensconced in the back of the car she could will herself to forget he was there.

She heard the rear door of the car open, but she did not look round. The books made a light thump on the back seat, and then the vehicle rocked to the greater weight of a human body. A hand reached down to the driver's door, and she turned to smile a welcome at Willy. It froze on her face as a brown arm with a white shirt sleeve rolled up past the elbow reached inside towards the steering wheel, and Reeve jackknifed himself into the driver's seat.

She would never have accepted the lift if she had known Reeve was going to drive. As Willy was the pilot, she had automatically supposed that he would take over this chore too. She simmered silently. The deep hide seat offered a refuge, and she shrank further back into it and turned her head mutinously towards the side window.

'I say!' An awestruck whistle came from Willy in the back seat. 'Does your uncle really read these things?' The titles of the books on the seat beside him were evidently too much for the pilot. A reluctant smile tilted Marion's lips. She herself was deeply interested in her uncle's work, but she had to admit that some of the tomes he used for reference made extremely hard reading.

'He's writing a book on road building through the ages,' she explained. The engine of the car made no more than a low purr, almost inaudible in the interior, and she found it easy to respond to the pilot in her normal voice. Different from the post van, she admitted to herself wryly. That worthy vehicle echoed every pothole in the road, and defeated reasonable conversation. 'He's ordered a special reference book from the library, and he'll be temporarily stuck without it. That's why I must go back into Dale End today. Otherwise I wouldn't have bothered,' she added deliberately.

She felt Reeve's eyes leave the road and slant towards her briefly, then away again, as if he had caught her hint that it was only the pressure of necessity that made her ride with him, and she felt an unrepentant satisfaction that her barb had gone home.

'Your uncle's research must make him appreciate the necessity for change,' he commented casually, apropos of nothing, and Marion turned her head and looked at him, puzzled.

'Change? What sort of change?'

'Any sort. Roads, where no roads were before....'

'But Uncle Miles is writing about Roman roads, not modern motorways,' Marion protested. She had not intended to speak to Reeve during the journey. The things she would have liked to say to him were better left unuttered, she thought grimly. But since Willy had broken the ice with a fairly innocuous topic of conversation, she responded, thankful despite herself to be able to ease the sense of strain that seemed to fairly crackle between herself and the man sitting beside her.

'Nevertheless, even the Romans must have disturbed the indigenous population by their road-building activities,' Reeve responded drily.

'I can't imagine a peasant population being consulted by an invading army,' Marion's tone was equally dry.

'Neither can I,' Reeve responded easily, 'but just the same, the desire to resist must have been there, the same as it would be today. The road-builders would automatically take the easier route, and that would mean cutting through the valleys, and consequently spoiling some of the best grazing land. The owners of the castles and the manor houses of the day wouldn't take kindly to having their flocks and herds disturbed.'

'But the roads brought benefits,' Marion argued. 'They encouraged trade, and opened up the country. If the peasants didn't see that, the lords of the manors should have done, surely?'

'I wonder if they did, at the time?' Reeve pondered. 'Afterwards, yes. Because ultimately they'd probably have built the roads themselves across the same routes, and thought the temporary upset to their pasture land a reasonable price to pay for what, when all the arguments were settled, would eventually come to be regarded as the greatest benefit to the greatest number of people.'

'Reeve's got your uncle's bent, he likes history,' Willy put in with an apologetic note from the back of the car.

Was it only that? Marion wondered. She felt, uneasily, that Reeve was trying to impress something on her. But what? A point of view? The subject of their conversation seemed innocent enough. It had arisen quite spontaneously, over a few chance library books. And yet his remarks held a subtle insistence she could not put her finger on. Was he a road-builder himself, perhaps? Maybe come to build a road through the valley, that would cause disruption to the people living there? She dismissed the idea as soon as it occurred to her. Fallbeck had nothing to attract a road-builder, even if he was one. The presence of Fallbeck Scar at the head of the valley had been sufficient, a few years ago, to take the new highway through Merevale. It was a broad, modern proof of sophisticated engineering, more than sufficient for the traffic it bore towards the distant motorways.

In spite of the logic of her argument, her sense of unease persisted. It followed her into the library, where Reeve dropped her with the explanation that he was going to take Willy to the airport. He made no mention of his own plans, and Marion did not ask.

'Thank you for the lift.'

She was stiffly polite. She did not consider she had

anything to thank him for. It was the result of his own deliberate action that had left her stranded in the first place.

'See you later,' Willy called from the back of the car, and Marion smiled and waved to him, and muttered between her teeth as she entered the cool quietude of the library.

'Much later. Back at the Fleece, in fact. . . .'

She would go back by the post van, she determined, and with her decision arrived at she could concentrate more easily on what she had come for. The book her uncle had ordered presented no problems, it was waiting for her on the shelf when she got in, but choosing the other books for him took some time. She dawdled over her task, browsing along the shelves, knowing the post van would not return to Fallbeck until late afternoon, and by the time she checked out her choice and was ready to leave, the clock above the desk at the entrance told her she had been there for over an hour.

She tucked the books under her arm and wished she had brought a bag in which to carry them. They seemed heavier than the ones she had brought back. She stepped outside and raised a dismayed face to the sky. Gone was the bright sunshine of the early morning. Cloud rolled in grey billows across the rooftops, and the pavement under her feet was shiny with wet. And she had with her neither jacket nor mac.

She half turned to go back into the library when she remembered it was their afternoon to close. A glance at her wrist watch told her that time would be in about ten minutes from now, so she could not return and sit reading in the hope that the weather would clear; neither could she, for much longer, remain in the shelter of the open doorway. She shivered. The rain had made it cold. Already a damp discomfort reminded her that toeless sandals were a poor protection against soaking wet pavements.

'I'll go and have some lunch.' She gave herself what comfort she could. She crouched back into the library door hurriedly as a sudden squall drove slanting wet across the street, and she turned concerned eyes on the burden in her arms. It would be bad enough if she got a soaking, but it could ruin the books.

'I'll wait until it eases off a bit, then go and buy a bag of some sort,' she decided. The books were more important than lunch, and they would be easier to carry in a bag. She was faced with an afternoon of walking round the stores, because the local cinema had gone the way of most such institutions, and was now converted into a bingo hall, effectively reducing her choice of activity on a wet day until the post van was ready for its evening run back to Fallbeck.

The squall slackened to a drizzle, and she stepped out of her temporary shelter just in front of the librarian, who turned the key in the old-fashioned lock with an air of finality, bade Marion a meticulous 'good afternoon'— it was exactly two minutes past twelve—and with a courteous nod left her wondering which route was best to the shops for the quickest shelter. A passing car sent up a shower of spray and she backed hastily away from the pavement edge, just as another vehicle drew to a halt beside her, and Reeve emerged from the driving seat.

'Jump in,' he bade her peremptorily, and wrenched open the door on the passenger side.

'I don't. . . .' Despite the weather, she drew back.

'If you don't mind getting wet yourself, at least give me the books,' he said impatiently. 'They're too valuable to be spoiled just because you choose to be stubborn.' He did not sound as if he cared whether she got drenched, so long as the books were safe, and her chin came up.

'I'm not being stubborn.'

'If you choose to get soaked rather than remain dry in the car, you're out of your mind,' he retorted bluntly, and before she could stop him he whisked the books out of her arms and into the rear seat. 'Are you going to get in or not?' he asked impatiently, and ducked his head against a return squall that flung itself against the shining coachwork in a hissing downpour. 'Make your mind up, quick. I'm getting wet as well as you.' He was still in his shirt sleeves, as unprotected as she was, and a tardy feeling of guilt made Marion duck into the shelter of the front passenger seat, and release him to run round the car to his own. He slammed the door on her with unnecessary force, indicative of the state of his feelings towards her, and she wondered what had made him return to pick her up. Perhaps he had not. He could have been passing, and seen her on the library steps, and stopped out of sheer compassion for her unprotected state—or concern for the books. She sent him a covert glance, and discovered he was watching her as he turned sideways in his seat, and brushed the clinging dampness from his shirt with undisguised irritation in his movements.

'If I get pneumonia, I shall expect you to nurse me,' he told her, and she flushed uncomfortably.

'I'm as wet as you are. Wetter.'

'I can see that.' He shook out the duster in his hand and re-balled it in a fresh grasp. 'Hold still, while I wipe you down. You needn't worry, it's quite clean,' as she made a wriggle of protest, 'and it'll take the surface wet off you at least.' His left hand grasped her shoulder while his right hand wielded the duster efficiently across her shoulders and collar, and over her hair—it seemed to linger on her hair, but perhaps that was merely her imagination—and across her face and chin, and finally she burst into indignant speech.

'I don't want a wash.'

'You look as if you've been under a shower bath,' he grinned. 'Sorry if I've spoiled your make-up.' He did not look in the least sorry. His eyes mocked her burning cheeks, and she snapped angrily,

'I don't use make-up.'

'That makes a nice change,' he said approvingly, and ignoring her glare he pushed the duster into her hands.

'You'd better mop up the rest yourself. Your legs and feet look pretty badly splashed.' They had caught most of the spray from the passing car, and were cold, and wet, and muddy. She would have liked to hurl his duster back at him, but sheer discomfort warned her that it would be wiser if she did as she was told. She gritted her teeth and bent to her task in silence, acutely aware of him watching her, noting her every movement.

'I'd have finished the job for you myself,' he murmured wickedly as she finished and sat back in her seat, 'but there's not much room to manoeuvre in a car.'

She looked round at him suspiciously, and then looked away again quickly.

'I'll wash the duster for you when we get home, and let you have it back,' she said hurriedly, and occupied herself with unnecessary concentration, folding the duster into neat halves, and then into quarters, rather than meet his look again.

'D'you need to do any shopping?' He keyed the engine into life and waited with his hand on the gear lever.

'No.' Marion ignored her need for a new sketching pencil. She would rather use the two broken halves of her old one than be under any further obligation to Reeve.

'In that case, we'll go and join Willy.'

She had not expected this. She thought he would be going straight back to Fallbeck, but of course he would have to pick up the pilot. She leaned back in her seat and resigned herself to Reeve's sole company until they got to the airport.

'We're a bit early,' he commented as they arrived. The journey did not seem so long as she thought it would be, principally because of the comfort of the large car. Reeve pulled into a parking slot alongside the white terminal building. 'We might as well go inside and wait,' he suggested, 'the observation lounge is less cramped than a car.' The Rover was far from cramped, but the observation lounge offered the prospect of other people, who would serve to distract her from the unwelcome awareness she felt at Reeve's close proximity. Perhaps take away the memory of the treacherous sweetness of his kiss the evening before, that insisted on returning despite her efforts to make it go away.

'Let's go and sit over by the window and have some lunch while we're waiting.' Before she could refuse, he spoke to a girl in staff uniform, and placing his hand under Marion's elbow he guided her towards a table beside the huge plate glass windows that walled one complete side of the lounge.

'What a wonderful view!' The activity on the ground captivated her attention, and made Reeve at least temporarily take second place. Two airliners were parked close to the terminal building, in the process of unloading their passengers, and she took the seat Reeve held out for her automatically, while she watched.

'Haven't you been here before?' Reeve asked her, and he sounded surprised. To Marion, his question sounded so much like the polite opening gambit of a strange partner at a dance—'do you come here often?'—that a reluctant smile lit her face.

'No, but I haven't had a lot of time really. I've only been back in the valley for about a year. This was still an Air Force station when I used to visit my aunt and uncle while I was small. It's only been a civilian airport for the last eight years or so.'

'And what made you neglect your relatives for the last eight years?'

'Art college at first.' Marion paused while the waitress brought their order—Reeve's order, he had not consulted her—and discovered she was hungry after all. The plate of smoked salmon in front of her, flanked by a bowl of crisp salad, and crusty rolls that felt hot to her touch, were an added appetiser, and she went on more readily, covering her initial awkwardness with conversation, 'Afterwards I had a stroke of luck that brought my work some recognition, so I've been able to freelance ever since, and several commissions have taken me abroad for quite long periods.'

She did not think it was necessary to add that the stroke of luck she referred to was in fact a coveted award won, not by luck, but by a piece of brilliant and original design work that brought her instant acclaim, and a request to submit her ideas from a firm that bore a world-famous name. Other such requests followed, and these gave her the opportunity to practise her talent while working where she pleased, and rapidly made her name known and respected in her particular field.

'So the Fleece isn't really your home?' Reeve looked thoughtful for some reason. It could have been that he was simply intent on dissecting his roll in order to butter it to his satisfaction. He did not look up when Marion replied.

'No, I came back to keep Uncle Miles company after my aunt died. We're all the family each other has got,' she explained somewhat inarticulately.

'He seems to be pretty well absorbed with his hobby, from what you said,' Reeve commented, 'and I must say it's a particularly interesting one.'

'He seems to live for it, these days,' Marion replied. 'Fortunately, running the Fleece these days doesn't make too many demands on him, and Mrs Pugh's an excellent manager. He seems content to leave her with it.'

'And you?' he queried, with a slight lift of his dark brows.

'I'm free to concentrate on my work again now, and—well—I suppose just be there.'

'For how long?' he asked softly.

'I haven't really given it any thought,' she answered him stiffly. It was no business of his why she was staying on at the Fleece, or for how long she chose to remain. 'The commission I'm working on at the moment may take some time, it's for a new building in the north of England. After that—who knows?' She shrugged. 'A lot of my work comes from overseas, and it's often more convenient to do it on site, with local materials. Where will the helicopter land when Willy brings it in?' She deliberately changed the subject.

'Over there, just past where those two airliners are parked. And he'll come in from that direction.' He gave her a keen glance, as if struck by her abrupt change of topic, but he made no reference to it, merely gestured towards a gap in the distant hills, that was the entrance to the Merevale valley, and the start of the gentler wold country those same hills gave way to further south.

So Willy had spent his morning flying over the valleys. Again. Why?

She turned impulsively to put the question to Reeve, and was interrupted by the arrival of a small band of people who entered through the double swing doors into the lounge, bringing with them a burst of chatter and laughter. Some were patently passengers from the two airliners parked on the tarmac. Marion identified a hat that she had seen descend from the one airplane. The article of millinery was eye-catching in colour, and she saw with an inward grimace, totally unsuitable for its wearer.

A group of men and women in uniform followed the passengers in, obviously the two crews, and they glanced across the tables near where Reeve and Marion were sitting to see if there were sufficient vacant seats to enable them to sit down together. They greeted the waitresses with cheerful familiarity, but although they must have seen Reeve and herself, none of them spoke as they took their places nearby. And surely, Marion thought, if Reeve belonged to one of the airlines using the airport, they would have known him, and acknowledged his presence?

CHAPTER FOUR

'This looks like Willy coming now.'

His voice penetrated Marion's preoccupation, and with an effort she brought her attention back to what he was saying. Something about Willy....

'Where?' She could see no sign of the pilot on the

flying field below the windows.

'Not on the field. Over there, look.' Reeve leaned across the narrow table, and caught her by the shoulder, turning her to face the gap in the hills. His hand stayed there, holding her, while he pointed with his other towards a faint speck in the sky, barely discernible as yet, it was so small.

'Over there, where that patch of blue sky is.' The clouds had spent their fury, and left a world refreshed, and ready to receive the strengthening sun again.

'You mean the helicopter.' She had only caught part of what he said. 'I thought you meant Willy himself.'

'The two are inseparable,' he told her drily.

His hand and her shoulder seemed to be the same. His palm felt hard and warm through the thin stuff of her blouse, and she moved uneasily, pulling away as much from the strange tremor that seemed to start from where his hand rested, and travel down the length of her spine, as from the slight restriction of his hold.

'We'd better go, or he'll wonder where we are.'

'There's no haste, Willy will be some time yet. He's got to wait for permission to land. There's plenty of time to finish your coffee in peace.'

He drank his own unhurriedly. Marion took a nervous gulp from her cup, and the hot black liquid steadied her. It ran warm fingers inside her, and took away some of the tremor, and she drained her cup, thankful that for once she had liberally sugared it. This man disturbed her, and she did not relish the feeling. He was an enigma, and she did not like enigmas.

'The helicopter's a lot closer.' The speck on the horizon was much bigger now, and rapidly increasing in size, although the double glazing on the windows ensured that no noise from it reached them. It loomed nearer, just as Reeve seemed to loom on her own horizon, she thought uneasily, slowly increasing his impact on her life, even beginning to dominate her thoughts.

'Let's go down and meet him.' She put a hasty check

on them, and jumped to her feet. The room that had seemed so large and airy before now suddenly seemed close and stuffy—confining. The gay talk and laughter of the passengers and the air crews became an unendurable noise.

'Stand well back, or you'll catch the down draught.' Reeve caught her hand in his own and held it as they reached the tarmac. As if she was a child, thought Marion indignantly, and then wondered suddenly if he was married. If he might be accustomed to holding a child's hand to prevent it from running forward, eager to see the helicopter. The thought brought a curious flatness with it. She wriggled her fingers, trying to force them from his grip, but it tightened instead, and a claustrophobic sense of capture made her temper flare.

'I can't reach my hanky out of my bag if you insist on gripping my fingers like a vice,' she told him icily.

He loosed her, and she fumbled in her bag with fingers which stung from the pressure of his hold. He gave her an oblique look, and stepped forward as the rotors of the machine swung to a stop. Marion remained where she was, under the overhang of the doorway from the terminal building, and Willy emerged from the cabin door of the helicopter.

'It's been a useful morning, Skipper,' he hailed Reeve as he rounded the tail of his machine, 'but it only confirms what we already know. It's an ideal site....'

Reeve said something to the pilot. Marion did not catch what it was, because he kept his voice pitched low, but she saw Willy raise his eyes to where she stood against the doorway, as if Reeve might have warned him that she was there, and within earshot. Warned him to be careful of what he said. There was the briefest of pauses, then Willy raised his hand to her, and called out cheerfully.

'Come and be introduced.' He patted the side of his machine, and reluctantly Marion followed Reeve. She did not particularly want to see the helicopter. At any other time she would have jumped at the chance, but now she felt all she wanted to do was to get back to the Fleece, and try and sort out the confusion that seemed to be tangling her mind into knots. She wished she had remained at home today, sketching, or working on her woodcut. Anything rather than be standing on the edge of the flying field invaded by doubts of she knew not what concerning the motives of the two men who were now guests at her uncle's hotel. And what else besides?

'Shan't keep you a minute,' the pilot called. 'I've just got to tie her down.'

'And feed her as well?' Marion laughed, thrusting her doubts aside.

'No, I mean it,' Willy said seriously. He moved round the machine to where the blade of the rotor protruded sideways, and slung a cord over it. The end looped over and dropped, and he jumped to catch it. Twice it eluded his fingers, his portly form was short, and his jump was not quite high enough.

'I'll get it.' Reeve jumped, too, but not very high, Marion noticed, and his longer arm caught the cord easily. He gave the end to Willy, who hooked it into a loop on the blade, and walking round to the back of the machine, drawing the rotor blade more or less in parallel with the body, he fastened the other end of the tether securely to the rear.

'How's that?' he beamed. 'Nicely hobbled, and guaranteed not to wander about on her own during the night.'

'I declare he treats that machine as if it was a human being,' Reeve laughed. He looked different when he smiled, Marion thought. The sternness vanished from his face, and he looked much younger. 'Come on, it's time we started back. You've eaten, I take it?' At least he seemed considerate of the subordinate, Marion chalked up a reluctant point in his favour.

'Would I be following you to the car if I hadn't?' Willy asked him cheerfully, and Marion chuckled. The answer was too obvious to need a reply. Reeve shot her an amused look, and his lips quirked upwards in a grin to match

Willy's, and it was in a much lighter atmosphere that they tucked themselves into the Rover and started back towards Fallbeck.

'You'll find some interesting literature on the back seat, to keep you occupied,' Reeve threw the information over his shoulder as he drove, and Willy groaned.

'Don't let him get on his hobbyhorse,' he warned Marion, 'turn him loose on your uncle, instead, they both talk the same language.'

'I wonder if we do?' The words were prosaic enough, it was the way he said them that made Marion cast him a sharp, sideways glance, but he was looking straight ahead, and there was nothing in his expression to indicate any ulterior meaning behind his remark. He appeared to be solely absorbed on the road ahead as the speedometer climbed to allow them to pass two coaches that were travelling in convoy, and then dropped back to a more moderate cruising speed once they were safely left behind.

'Stop it!' Marion chided herself. She was beginning to look for a brigand behind every bush. If she dissected every word Reeve spoke to find what lay behind it, there would be no ending to it.

'Thank you for the lift.' She said it sincerely this time. She had unexpectedly enjoyed the ride back in the car, and she turned to receive her library books from Willy.

'I'll take those, they're heavy,' Reeve forestalled her.

'I'll put the car away.' Willy manipulated himself into the driving seat, and Marion waited beside Reeve until the big car slid away towards the converted stables at the back of the hotel, which gave more than adequate accommodation for whatever vehicles might need them. The brake lights winked briefly as the Rover turned the corner and vanished, and with its disappearance Marion became conscious once again of the sense of strain between herself and Reeve, like a heavy cloud hovering, now that Willy had left them alone.

'I can manage the books, I haven't got to carry them far.' Once inside the house she could escape to their own quarters, and Reeve could do what he pleased, she thought thankfully.

'In that case I might as well keep them, and carry them in,' Reeve denied her blandly, and short of physical force she could not very well remove the books from his arms. 'You can take this, though,' he handed her a buff business envelope. The top was open, and without thinking, Marion peeped inside.

'My hairband....' She raised surprised eyes to his face.

'Your drawing's there as well,' Reeve told her drily. 'You do seem to leave your property scattered in the most unlikely places,' he criticised, and her cheeks flamed. It was his fault she had left her belongings behind. Both times. The first time she had fled from a shadow, and her colour darkened at the memory of it. The second time she had fled from his kiss. And she could not remind him of that. She bit back the hot words that flooded her lips.

'Did you get the book I ordered, my dear?' Miles Dorman crossed the hall just as she and Reeve came through the door together, and saved her from having to reply. 'Ah, I see you did,' his eyes alighted on the volumes in Reeve's arms.

'You're lucky with this one, sir,' Reeve put down his burden on the hall table, and slid open the cover of the topmost book. 'It's the recently revised edition. I've got the earlier one myself, but this one is supposed to be much more informative from about,' he flicked the pages over, 'from about 1286 onwards.'

'Mr Harland's interested in history too,' Marion put in tautly, and Reeve paused in his inspection of the book.

'Call me Reeve,' he bade her, 'it's much easier.' He turned to her uncle. 'Marion told me about the work you're engaged on,' he said, and Marion's lips tightened.

I suppose because he's told me to use his Christian name, he thinks it gives him the right to use mine, she fumed silently, but there was nothing she could do about it now.

'Marion's helped me a great deal,' Miles Dorman was speaking, 'but if you're interested in my work, why don't you join us after dinner tonight, and we could talk about it,' he invited eagerly.

'Oh, no!' Marion groaned beneath her breath. It was bad enough having Reeve beneath the same roof as a guest, without having to endure his presence in their private living quarters as well.

'We won't....' She started to say 'We won't have time tonight,' and then she caught sight of her uncle's face. It was bright with the seldom experienced pleasure of meeting a fellow being who was interested in his somewhat abstruse subject, and the words died on her lips. Miles Dorman, with his white hair and slight, stooping figure, was more of a historian by nature than a hotel proprietor.

'We won't be having dinner until after seven,' she changed her sentence hurriedly, 'so any time after about eight will do. Unless, of course, you've got other plans for this evening?' she asked hopefully.

'Not at the moment.' His look challenged her, leaving her to wonder at what other plans he might have in mind. And who else they might include.

'Bring your friend, too, if he's interested,' Miles Dorman extended his invitation, and Marion's gloom lightened a little. With Willy there to chat to, it might not be so bad. She could leave Reeve exclusively to her uncle.

'I'll tell Willy you asked,' Reeve said politely, 'I'm sure he'll be pleased, but he's got a report to write that will take him most of the evening,' he neatly foiled her half formed plans.

'In that case we won't disturb him, of course.' Miles Dorman could not imagine a worse fate than to be disturbed at his writing, even for meals. Mrs Pugh had a daily battle to keep him adequately fed, but Marion did not imagine Willy shared her uncle's dedication. She had a sudden impulse to invite the pilot herself, but that, too, died half formed. If Reeve had spoken the truth and Willy really had got a report to write, perhaps about his flight over the valleys that morning, her own intervention might get Willy into trouble if he accepted the offer of an evening with the family, as she suspected he would, and neglect his paper work. She liked the pilot, and it would not be fair to sour his relationship with his superior—employer? She did not know which, and the lack of knowledge irritated her. But Willy had his job to look after, and he would have to put up with Reeve long after they left the hotel. Reluctantly she decided to leave things as they were, and live through the evening as best she could.

She made an excuse and ran upstairs to her own room to change. Despite her attentions with Reeve's duster in the car, her stockings were still mud-splashed, and felt uncomfortably grubby. The feeling brought her mind back to the promise to wash the duster for him. She showered and changed, and washed stockings and duster together. It would dry on the rack over the kitchen range, and she could iron it and give it back to him after dinner.

She creased her forehead at the thought of after dinner. It looked as if it was going to be a difficult evening. Although if Reeve and her uncle intended to delve into the new reference books she had brought from the library, it would leave her free to do something else herself. Perhaps finish her sketch. She turned to where she had tossed the buff-coloured envelope Reeve had given her on to her bed. At least he had the decency to keep her sketch flat. She picked up the envelope, suddenly curious. It was a business envelope, the sort that usually had a firm's name and address printed on the back. It might give her a clue to Reeve's firm, and from that, to what he himself was doing in the valley. Her brief excitement flickered out when she saw that the flap of the envelope had been removed, leaving just the open ended receptacle which—she turned it over—was bare of any marking that might provide her with a useful clue.

Tipping it up made the hairband slip out, and the drawing followed it. And something flat and hard followed

that. She frowned, and reached down on to the counterpane to pick it up. It was a box. Instant recognition came
as she turned it over. The flat cardboard container held
quality sketching pencils—the kind she always provided
for herself, she enjoyed working with good tools, but her
indulgence told her they were costly. And there was a box
full. She flipped the lid open. Two dozen, of assorted
numbers. She ran fingers along the line. Two of each
number, and four of the most popular one—the one she
had stepped on, and broken.

'He can have them back!' she exclaimed angrily. Willy
must have mentioned to him that she had broken her
pencil when she stepped on it, and this was his reply—an
arrogant presentation of two dozen of the very best leads
obtainable. Like tossing pennies to the rabble, she thought
angrily. She felt strongly tempted to put them on his
dressing table in the next room, then she paused. He might
retaliate by simply returning them in the same way. Stalemate. It would be better if she gave them back to him
herself, with a dignified refusal, and returned his duster at
the same time.

She ironed the check square into neat folds and took it
with her, and the box of pencils, into their private sitting
room, along with the coffee tray, when dinner was over.
Thank goodness Mrs Pugh lived *en famille*. She was relieved to see the amiable little housekeeper already ensconced on the settee with her knitting.

'A sweater?' Marion asked.

'A cardigan for your uncle,' Mrs Pugh replied, absentmindedly, one needle busy counting up the number of rows
she had already done. 'Twenty-three, twenty-four, twenty-
five—there, that's the welt done, it's all plain knitting now
up to the armholes. His other's giving at the elbows,' she
said by way of explanation, 'your aunt was in no fit state
to keep an eye on his clothes, and they're beginning to need
looking over.'

'Does he need suits, or anything?' Marion knew how
absentminded her uncle could be about such matters. She

should have thought of it herself, she realised guiltily.

'Dearie me no, it's only his sweaters, and you can safely leave them with me,' Mrs Pugh smiled. 'It'll be nice for your uncle to have Mr Harland to talk to about his roads and things,' she added complacently.

Nice for her uncle, but Marion had reservations about herself. If they lived in an area where there was some-where to go, she would have made an excuse to go out, but there was nowhere in Fallbeck to offer a convenient escape route. She resigned herself to the inevitable, and began to pour coffee as her uncle and Reeve came in to-gether, the older man showing an animation she had not seen for a long time.

'You'd be surprised how much clearer it is from the air.' Reeve paused in what he was saying to receive his coffee from Marion with a nod of thanks, and walked over to sit opposite to her uncle across the fireplace. There was a small fire smouldering in the grate, just enough to combat the chill caused by the earlier rain. Marion watched him go with an odd sense of pique. She had come downstairs ready to do battle over the box of pencils, and he seemed hardly to notice she was there. He stretched out in his chair and carried on talking to her uncle. She tried not to listen, but his voice seemed to command her attention, although he was not talking to her.

'Configurations show up much more clearly from above. Lines and ridges, and the overall shape of things that may not be obvious when viewed from eye level, become a coherent pattern if they're looked at from the air. There's the line of an old road or track of some sort crossing the hills here, I noticed it while we were travelling above them the other day.'

'There's an old drovers' road hereabouts,' Miles Dorman answered him eagerly. 'It's never been possible to trace the entire route of it. Bits of it are known, but they peter out, and the rest has had to be guessed at by piercing to-gether knowledge and assumption.'

'You must come up with Willy and me in the 'copter one

day and have a look for yourself,' Reeve urged him. 'The evidence of the road that I saw seemed faitly conclusive, and it ran for a number of miles without a break, although it was much fainter here and there. That's where you'd lose track of it, I expect, trying to follow it from ground level, but if you agree to fly with us you may be able to log the missing bits, if you've got a map?'

'Indeed I will, at the first opportunity.' The older man could not believe his good fortune, and showed it. His face was as eager as a child's.

'It makes a difference, doesn't it?' Mrs Pugh spoke softly from beside Marion. 'Having someone to share with, I mean?'

'All the difference in the world,' Marion agreed reluctantly. Her uncle looked years younger, and she should have felt grateful to Reeve. One part of her did, but the other part watched him suspiciously, with the uneasy feeling that for some reason best known to himself, he was making up to her uncle, using their mutual interest as a lever to gain the other man's trust. There was no doubt that Reeve's interest in her uncle's subject was genuine, he was almost as knowledgeable as his host.

'He sounds a bit like an archaeologist,' Mrs Pugh suggested *sotto voce* from beside her.

'He seems to know a lot about it,' Marion felt herself relax. If Reeve was an archaeologist, it would explain a great deal, although—she wrinkled her forehead, trying to remember what it was the pilot said when he jumped out of his machine at the airport. 'It's an ideal site.' Surely archaeologists called them 'digs', not sites? But perhaps a 'dig' was after they had started excavating whatever it was they were looking for, not before? She gave up the unequal struggle and tried to concentrate on finishing her sketch.

'I haven't seen that one before.' Mrs Pugh forsook her knitting for a moment to peer over the tops of her spectacles to see what it was she was drawing. 'Is that the one you did on the fell? Why, that was the day we saw your helicopter for the first time, Mr Harland,' she remembered.

Marion tensed. Would Reeve comment on her craven behaviour on the fell? She sent him a look that was unconsciously appealing. He met it, but she could not read the expression in his eyes. They were darkly shadowed in the evening dusk of the low-beamed room. Hooded by the shadows, like the eyes of a bird of prey. Dark pools, of an unknown depth, into which she dared not dabble for fear she might drown....

'It's time we had the light on.' She jumped to her feet, spilling the pencil from her lap. It was the longer half of the broken one, resharpened, and shorter than she liked it, but she would rather put up with that than use one from the box Reeve had given to her. She clicked the light into instant brilliance, dispelling the shadows, and she turned back towards the settee as Reeve bent to pick up her pencil. He looked at it, balanced it in his palm, deducing from its size which pencil it was she was using, and why she was using it. And then he straightened up and looked at her, and his eyes were hard, like steel, challenging her refusal of the gift. Telling her that she would accept it, because he said so. She faced him defiantly, felt the force of his will as his eyes locked with her own, and determined not to give way.

'Is that a short pencil, my dear? I could do with one, I've used all the others you let me have.' Her uncle smiled and took it from Reeve's hand. 'I use up Marion's short pencils, they're ideal for map-making,' he explained. 'Have you got plenty yourself?' he asked her, always considerate.

'She had a new box from Dale End this morning.' Reeve spoke deliberately into the silence, answering for her. He addressed her uncle, but his eyes held Marion's, deliberately imposing his will on her own; forcing her into a position where she would have no option but to accept his gift, and use it. He did not say he had bought the pencils for her, even through the hot surge of anger that consumed her, she noticed that.

'In that case, I shan't be depriving you. I don't like long pencils myself, they get in the way.' Miles Dorman foiled her half-formed decision to give her uncle the whole box full of new ones. 'I meant to ask you to shade in this map for me,' he went on, and unrolled a piece of parchment and spread it flat on the table. 'You do it so much better than I can. It's just this piece here, where the final length of road is marked.' He traced a roughly drawn line across the parchment.

'I'll do it for you now.' Marion held out her hand for the half pencil. If she could get it back she would give her uncle the whole new box full after all, she could split them in two for him to use. It would give her the greatest pleasure to break them all, she thought vindictively.

'Try out one of your new ones instead.' Reeve picked up the box from where she had dropped it, along with the duster, on the settee, and flipped open the lid, offering it to her like an open packet of cigarettes. Daring her to refuse to take one.

'It'll save me from being held up if you can finish the map for me now,' her uncle said gratefully, and slid the half pencil into the top pocket of his jacket. 'I'll sharpen your new one for you.' He took one from the box Reeve held out. 'Will this number do?'

Marion nodded, dumbly. She felt incapable of speaking. She watched while he sharpened it to a keener end for her, and abruptly turned her back on Reeve when her uncle held it out to her. She took it. It seemed to burn her fingers when she touched it, and she bent over the map, blotting out the sight of the dark, hawk face watching her. The rough sketched line of the road wavered before her eyes, and it took all her willpower to set to work to shade the area to the depth she knew from experience her uncle would desire. She could feel Reeve standing over her, although her eyes were bent on the map, his inflexible determination reached her like a spoken command, which he meant her to obey.

'I'll finish off the finer bits for you tomorrow, in the daylight.' It was impossible for her to do the map justice with Reeve there, his presence destroyed her concentration as well as her will power, and she straightened up with an impatient sigh.

'This is part of the drovers' road you can see from the fells by Fallbeck Scar.' To her relief her uncle made no comment on her reluctance to finish the map right away. Instead he turned the parchment round so that Reeve could see it more clearly. 'I'm not too certain about this end bit, though. I drew that from memory, and thinking back I'm almost sure it should be shown towards the right of that rocky outcrop there, not towards the left.'

'I'll take it with me tomorrow,' Marion offered, 'if it's fine I'll be going up the fell to try and finish off my own sketch. What with one thing and another I didn't manage to finish it today.' She gave Reeve a resentful stare, but he met it coolly and she turned away. 'I can do any alterations to the map for you while I'm up there.'

'Why not take Reeve with you?' Miles Dorman suggested innocently. 'He's seen the road from the air, he might like to see it at closer quarters.'

'I can make sure your map's marked up properly,' Reeve accepted his offer blandly, and Marion's temper flared.

'I'm quite capable of map drawing, I've done it before.' And I've no intention of allowing you to check my work, she added silently. 'Besides, I shall be busy finishing my own sketch,' she went on out loud, and Reeve said smoothly,

'I shan't disturb you.'

That was just the trouble. He did disturb her. Just by being there he took away her poise and the calm stability that until now she had always taken for granted. Until now, nobody had been able to upset it.

'I'll have to disturb myself,' Miles Dorman said regretfully, 'I always spend the last half hour or so with Jim in the bar. It helps ensure we close on time with no argu-

ment,' he smiled, and Marion wondered, not for the first
time, how it was the scholarly little man came to be in
such an unlikely trade. Her aunt had had the business
acumen, which probably accounted for it.

'I'll come and see to any bits of washing up that are
left,' Mrs Pugh folded up her knitting unhurriedly. 'There's
never very much these days,' she said regretfully, 'I mind
the time when we had a bus service, the place used to be
busy all the evening.'

'I'll come and help you,' Marion offered hurriedly. The
last thing she wanted was to be left alone with Reeve.

'There's no need,' Mrs Pugh was maddeningly obtuse.
'There'll only be a few glasses left to wash, I expect. Jim
will have done the rest.' And she turned and followed
Miles Dorman out of the room.

'And then there were two,' Reeve quoted softly, into
the crackling silence that followed their departure.

She picked up the map from the table, keeping her back
towards him. She did not want to turn to face him. Her
hands trembled, so that the papers rustled, and she jostled
them together, making believe she was trying to straighten
them, to cover up the reason for the sound. If he had got
any sense of decency, she thought desperately, he would
go away and leave her alone. She turned from the table to
the settee, and all the while she was acutely aware of him,
watching her. Her sketch lay where she had left it, and she
put the half-finished map on top, ready for the morning.
Why did her uncle have to suggest Reeve should accom-
pany her on the fell? she asked herself crossly. Maybe it
would rain, and they would not be able to go. The thought
gave her a momentary crumb of comfort.

The small chore done, there was no further excuse to remain facing the settee. But the alternative was to turn
and face Reeve. She knew without looking that he had not
moved from where he stood. She picked up the map and
her sketch and hesitated. The box of pencils still lay on
the cushions. Her lips tightened. They could remain
there, so far as she was concerned. Her eyes fell on the

neatly folded duster beside them. She had come downstairs intending to return them both to Reeve. Now was her opportunity. The duster was nearer to her hand, and she braced herself and picked it up.

'It's freshly washed and ironed.' She held it out towards him, and spoke through stiff lips. Her body felt tense, like a bow string, and she was strangely grateful for the tension, she felt if it left her she would begin to shake, and Reeve would see. Her breath came hurriedly, shallow and unsatisfying, and nearly stopped when he bent and reached for the box of pencils from the settee cushions.

'You've forgotten these.'

Stalemate. The thought flashed across her mind without humour. Somewhere it seemed to have occurred to her before, but she could not think where.

'I'll take this.' He took the duster from her nerveless fingers. 'And you,' his voice hardened with inflexible determination, 'you will take these.' He folded her fingers that had held the duster, firmly over the flat box of pencils, and his own held them there, forcing her to grip it; feeling the sharp edge of the box that began to press into the palm of her hand, with a discomfort that would soon become pain.

'And if you don't feel like thanking me for the pencils,' he went on in an even voice, 'that won't stop me from thanking you for the duster. Thanking you properly,' he mimicked Mrs Pugh. With his one hand still over her own, forcing her to keep her grip on the pencil box, he drew her towards him. He put his other hand round her waist, she could feel the palm of it warm against her back, as she had felt it warm on her shoulder in the airport observation lounge. His touch seemed to take away her power to move, to breathe....

With silent fascination, she watched his face come closer to her own, waited for the pressure of his lips that she knew would come, anticipating the heady sweetness that would course like old wine through her veins. The tension left her, and she began to tremble, and his lips found hers, touching them masterfully, but at the same time gently, tasting the sweetness of them as a connoisseur tastes fine wine.

Something deep and unsuspected inside her came to life at the ardour of his touch. Emotions that until now had lain dormant, flowered into tender bloom as his lips began to wander, travelling over her eyes, closing each lid in turn, then passing on across the delicate blue veins of her throbbing temples, down across the slender line of her jaw, until they came to rest in the warm, pulsing hollow of her throat. Their touch acted like a golden key, releasing emotions that had lain prisoner for too long. She drew a long shuddering breath, and her arms rose, clasping him round his neck, her hands drawing down his dark head hungrily to her own again when he raised it for an instant to look deep into her eyes.

'Marion!'

The dying embers of the fire made soft shadows on the wall. They flickered like tiny smiles across the ash, as the log burned through at last, and crumbled into the bottom of the grate with a sound like a sigh. The momentarily stronger flame threw into relief two shadows, and died shyly away as the two became blended into one, and first the duster, then the box of pencils, dropped unnoticed on to the floor.

CHAPTER FIVE

PERHAPS it was raining.

Marion jumped hopefully out of bed and pulled aside the curtains, and her heart sank. A light morning mist shrouded the hills, thickening as it neared the valley and the line of the beck, but already the sun was busy dispelling it from the nearer slopes, fulfilling its promise of a perfect day. There seemed to be no way she could escape spending it with Reeve. Her uncle had irretrievably committed her last night. She shook her head impatiently. She did not want to remember last night. Her cheeks burned at the thought of Reeve, and how he must be laughing at her now.

'He's won Uncle Miles over, now I suppose he thinks he's won me as well,' she derided herself bitterly. Just what he might want to win her over to escaped her. It all seemed to be bound up in the inexplicable mystery of Reeve himself, and why he had come to the valley.

'He'll find this morning I'm a different proposition,' she vowed to herself, and her lips set determinedly. If Reeve thought he could gain her trust by a few casually dispensed kisses in the firelight, he could think again.

But had they been so casual, to her?

'Of course they were,' she assured herself aloud, and forcefully, as if hearing herself speak might serve to convince her. A flash of temper, a clash of wills, and manlike Reeve had chosen that way to settle it, to get his own way. She tried to ignore the fact that her own feelings would not settle down. The unexpected emotions his kisses roused in her would not return dutifully to hibernation again, and she felt disturbed, and restless, and angry with Reeve because of it. Why, oh, why had Uncle Miles suggested Reeve go with her today? But despite her anger against Reeve, she could not find it in her heart to vent her feelings on her scholarly relative, particularly when he told her amiably,

'I've sharpened two more of those new pencils for you. You left them in the sitting room last night.' He handed them to her in the hall on her way out, and she accepted them in silence and tucked them inside the rubber band stretched round her clipboard.

'I've got your map.' To be on the safe side she slipped a waterproof cover over the block of papers. The weather could change with dramatic suddenness on the high tops, and her uncle's parchment was precious.

'I'll carry that for you.' Reeve appeared and held out

his hand, but she clung to her clipboard stubbornly.

'It's not heavy. Besides, you've got your letters to carry.' To her relief he did not insist, he merely nodded and said,

'I'll drop these in at the Post Office on our way out, they'll go by the next delivery.'

'That won't be until this evening, the post van's already gone this morning.' She felt a malicious satisfaction that in this one thing, at least, Reeve could not have his own way.

'No matter, there's no great urgency,' he spoiled her slight triumph. 'If there had been, Willy would have taken them with him into Dale End.'

'Aren't you going with him?' She grasped at the final straw. Perhaps after all he might change his mind about coming with her.

'I promised to come with you, remember?' He eyed her quizzically, and she felt her colour rise.

'In that case let's go. It's a long climb,' she told him shortly.

'The Post Office first,' he insisted, and she followed him reluctantly. She would have preferred to walk on and assert her independence, and let him catch up with her as best he might, but she wanted a packet of paper handkerchiefs. They would have formed part of her shopping yesterday afternoon if the rain, and Reeve, had not prevented her from doing any. A rising sense of irritation took her at the seeming inevitability of it all. Even the weather conspired to throw her into Reeve's company.

Her irritation rose still further as she stepped into the tiny overcrowded shop and saw Zilla Wade already at the counter, deep in conversation with the postmistress. The advent of other customers did not check the farmer's wife's diatribe, if anything it served to increase its venom.

'It's disgraceful, that's what it is. First they stopped the bus service, and now it's the Post Office.' She caught sight of Marion, and her sharp black eyes glowed spitefully. 'They'll be taking the licence off the Fleece next, you mark my words. And then what?' she asked the world at large, not giving it time to answer before she went on, the words tumbling over one another in bitter recrimination, 'it's the only place the menfolk have got round here, it's bad enough trying to scrape a living off the holding, goodness knows, without having nowhere to go at the end of the day,' she cried.

'There's Dale End,' the postmistress put in timidly, and the farmer's wife snorted.

'Dale End takes time, and gas costs money, and we've got neither to spare. We have to work for our living.' The last, Marion knew, was aimed at herself. Zilla Wade had made plain her opinion of art as a livelihood on more than one occasion. She ignored the jibe, and approached the counter.

'I've heard nothing about the Fleece losing its licence. I'm sure Uncle Miles would have told me, if he had.' She wondered, uneasily, if he would. If, indeed, these days he would even have bothered to open the notification in the first place, but she suppressed her doubts, conscious of Zilla Wade's sharp eyes on her face, noting her every change of expression, and ready to make capital out of it.

'The Post Office hasn't taken away my licence yet,' the postmistress recovered her courage under Marion's smile, and spoke more firmly. 'They only said they'd have to consider it, because there's so few folk in Fallbeck who need it now.'

'That will make a difference to your trade, won't it?' Reeve spoke sympathetically.

'It won't be worth keeping open just to sell a few sweets and birthday cards,' the white-haired woman agreed, and her lips trembled. 'I could go and live with our Brenda in Dale End, I suppose, she keeps on at me to go. She's got a big house, and I could have a couple of rooms of my own, and take my bits and pieces, but I don't know ... it's the upheaval, and all.'

"Perhaps it won't come to that after all,' Reeve said kindly, and passed his letters over the counter. One was a long package. Willy's report? Marion edged closer to try and see the address to which it was being sent, but Reeve turned the package the other way round so that the writing was upside down from where she stood, and she could make no sense of the letters. The postmistress put out her hand to take them, and Marion moved away again, and pretended to be intent on picking out her packet of paper handkerchiefs.

'I'll take a couple of packets of chocolate while we're here,' Reeve delved deep into his pocket and picked up two of the largest slabs of fruit and nut chocolate from the counter.

'Fancy stuff's no good for you,' Zilla Wade sniffed critically, but the eyes of the little postmistress brightened.

'This is how it used to be, when we had a bus service,' she said wistfully, and handed him his change.

'The lady looked as if a bit of sweet stuff might not come amiss with her,' Reeve remarked ruefully on their way out.

'It'll melt in this heat,' Marion predicted unkindly. She could not bring herself to agree with him out loud, though she doubted if chocolate would do much to sweeten Zilla Wade's tongue.

'We'll eat it.'

'You'll die of thirst, eating sweet stuff when you're climbing. It's getting hot already.'

'In that case, I'll donate it to a worthy cause,' Reeve said imperturbably, and taking her by the arm he crossed the street towards the school where John Cornish was ushering his pitifully small class through the gate.

'I seem to have acquired two surplus blocks of chocolate,' he smiled at the older man. He had an unexpectedly sweet smile. Marion tried not to notice, but she could not help herself. It lit his eyes, and warmed them, curved the clean-cut lips, and softened the stern set of the darkly tanned face. 'I thought perhaps you might find a good home for them,' his glance rested on the suddenly hopeful faces of the children.

'Indeed we can,' John Cornish accepted the unexpected windfall delightedly. 'Two of my class have got birthdays today, we'll have a little party.'

Now he's made another conquest—the thought flashed across Marion's mind. He's won over John Cornish, and his entire class. And that probably means the children's parents as well. There was no reason why Reeve should not be nice to the people he met in the village. And it was her fault that he had jettisoned the chocolate, she had goaded him into it, but the knowledge left her unrepentant, and still suspicious. She wished she knew his motive for coming to Fallbeck in the first place. He was obviously not there merely on holiday, and if he had come to the area on business, then surely Dale End would have been a more logical place in which to stay.

'Is that his entire school?' Reeve asked her casually as they moved away, and Marion answered him absentmindedly, her thoughts still on the conundrum of why he had come to the valley.

'Mmm. It'll be smaller still soon, when the children over eleven years old leave to go to Dale End. There's two sets of twins going, which won't help.'

'How do they get to Dale End, without a bus service?'

'By the post van, of course.' How else did he think they got there? she thought impatiently. 'They go first thing in the morning, and back at night. It makes a long day for them, but there's no alternative.'

'What about the winter, when it snows? How do they get on about schooling then?' Reeve persisted, and Marion frowned.

'The education authorities have thought that one out, too,' she told him drily. Simply because Fallbeck was isolated, it did not automatically mean that they were devoid of intelligence, she thought sarcastically. 'During the worst of the winter the children board in Dale End. The pass gets blocked if we have a lot of snow, and it's better for them to stay with families in the town rather than risk the journey, or lose their lessons.'

'That can't be very satisfactory from the parents' point of view,' Reeve commented. 'I don't think I'd like my children in the care of strangers for most of the week. There'd be no family life left.'

His children? So that meant he was married. She stiffened. If Reeve was married he had had no right to kiss her last night. And she had no right to respond. Marion abhorred disloyalty. Marriage was for ever.... Her voice was icy when she replied.

'There can't be a lot of family life if the husband is away most of the time,' she pointed out coldly. 'But I suppose it's different, for you?' He pronounced on the rest of the world, she thought angrily, and calmly ignored his own dereliction. He had been at the Fleece for several days now, and showed no signs of leaving, so what was happening to his own family life in the meantime?

'Since I have neither wife nor children, it doesn't apply to me.'

He was laughing at her. His eyes, narrowed with amusement, watched her, reading her thoughts. Knowing she remembered last night's kiss, and sensing accurately the desolate feeling of betrayal that swept over her when she thought he was married.

Speechless with embarrassment, she cast about her desperately for something—anything—to break the charged silence between them. A dog-collared figure emerged from the church and turned into the gateway of a nearby cottage.

'Good morning, Vicar!' Marion waved gaily, and received an answering greeting, and Reeve said,

'I haven't been inside the church yet. What's it like?'

'Architecturally, it's uninteresting,' Marion said curtly, repeating what she had often heard her uncle say to visitors. They had already made one stop at the Post Office, and another at the school, both for Reeve's benefit. If she had been by herself she could have been half way up the fellside by now, while it was still cool enough to make climbing comfortable. As it was the sun was rapidly getting hotter, and it would be a sticky climb before they got to the top. If Reeve had got nothing better to do than stroll about inspecting the village, she had, she told herself resentfully. There was her own sketch to finish, and her uncle's map. She was determined Reeve should not touch her uncle's map. His arrogant assumption that he was more capable of placing the course of the drovers' road than she still nettled her.

'In that case, another day will do.'

Reeve was maddeningly indifferent. In her present mood Marion felt she would almost have welcomed opposition from him, if only to give her an opportunity to fight back. She set her lips and turned upwards, off the road, and blessed the fact that the sheep-tracks across the fellside were narrow. That way, she would not have to walk beside Reeve. Then she realised he would have to walk behind her, and that was even worse. Deliberately she increased her pace, intent on leaving him behind. Since she had returned to Fallbeck she had spent a good deal of her time walking the fells, her slender figure made light of the slopes, and her breathing was scarcely quickened by the time she paused half way up, where the track forked, to decide which path to take.

The clink of a stone just below her made her start. Her deliberate burst of speed should have left Reeve well below her. Instead, he was only about a yard away, and climbing easily. She noticed to her chagrin that his breathing, too, was easy and unhurried. And the laughter in his eyes told her he knew why she had quickened her pace upwards, and because of it he had deliberately quickened his own to checkmate her move.

She compressed her lips and willed herself to remain where she was, looking at the view. It was from about this spot she had first caught sight of Ben Wade and his dog when she was last on the hill. The small flock of sheep was still in the field where he had penned them, and it was obvious that they had not yet settled down to their new surroundings. They moved restlessly, grazing spasmodically, and raising their voices in repeated calling.

'They're kicking up quite a racket,' Reeve commented, following the direction of her gaze. 'The others seem quiet enough.' His keen glance roved the hillside.

'Ben Wade only brought them here the other day. He bought them from a holding in Merevale,' Marion told him. 'The farmer there is giving up for some reason, and Ben was glad to take some of his stock off his hands at a cheap rate. The Wades can't resist a bargain,' she said drily, 'that was Zilla Wade—Ben's mother—you saw in the Post Office this morning.'

Her lips curved upwards at his expression, and suddenly she found she was laughing with him; tilting back her head and letting the warm breeze riffle soft fingers through her hair, and chuckling at unspoken, shared thoughts, that both knew, and neither wanted to utter. 'They'll quieten soon enough,' she sobered again, 'it's being in a strange pasture that makes them cry, as soon as they get used to it they'll settle down. Sheep are like that.'

'So are people,' Reeve remarked unexpectedly, and Marion looked at him sharply. He had a way of making odd, unrelated comments that she found disconcerting. It was as if there was some deep, underlying meaning, that she did not understand, and it had the effect of leaving her uneasy in her mind.

'Let's get on.' She turned abruptly and moved upwards again, but her pace was slower now, and when the bracken and heather began to thin, giving way to sparse turf and rock, Reeve moved up and walked beside her. They reached the ridge in silence, and Marion turned along it, seeking the rock where she had sheltered before. And from where the helicopter had flushed her like a frightened quail. She smarted at the memory.

'This is as far as I go.' She dropped on to the patch of turf beside the rock. Reeve could do whatever he liked, she thought mutinously. She did not invite him to come with her, and she did not feel obliged to entertain him now he was here. The hare had gone, of course, and with two people moving about it was unlikely it would come back. If she had been on her own, it might have done, she thought resentfully. But the clump of harebells was there, exactly as she had started to sketch it, and left off to draw the hare while she had the opportunity. She stripped the waterproof cover from her clipboard. She felt Reeve's eyes on the pencils, and shrugged. She would have to use them now, she had no others with her.

'While you're finishing your sketch, I'll do the map for you.' He leaned nonchalantly against the rock and reached down to remove the map from under the clip.

'No!' She covered it with her hands, gripping the edge of the clipboard with knuckles that showed white. 'I'll do it myself, I'm quite capable,' she told him in a taut voice.

'Please yourself.' He straightened up and shaded his eyes with one hand, looking across the sunlit fellside. 'Is that the rock over there, where your uncle marked the drovers' road?' he asked interestedly, and she relaxed, and let her hand fall away from the clipboard.

'Yes, I'll go over there afterwards and make sure which side of the rock it runs. It'll be simple enough to alter the marking on the map if it's necessary,' she added firmly.

'I'll borrow it to guide me in the meantime.' Before she realised what he was about to do, he leaned down again, lithely bending from the waist in an effortless movement, and took the clipboard from her hands, and deftly removed the map from beneath the clip, leaving her sketch where it was.

'I told you. . . .' She went white with fury, and he gazed at her coolly.

'I know what you told me, and I won't mark your map,' he said smoothly. 'I merely want to borrow it for a moment to guide me in the right direction. That's what maps are made for,' he taunted her softly. 'Now I'll leave you in peace to get on with your sketch.' And he walked away, with the map in his hand.

'You—you——' she breathed chokingly. She stood rigid against the rock, and hated him with a force that frightened her. She glared at his retreating back, and wondered if he could feel her loathing, as she had felt his look from the helicopter when she descended the hillside. But if he did he gave no sign. He paused once, but he did not turn to look back. She saw him straighten the parchment in his hands, holding it flat against the tug of the light breeze, and then he looked away downhill towards the rocky outcrop, as if comparing it with the map, and debating on which side of the rock the line of the drovers' road ran.

'I don't care what he says, I'll decide for myself, so he's only wasting his time,' she muttered rebelliously. She sat down on the turf and reached for her sketchblock. 'He can wander as far away as he likes, I don't care so long as he leaves me in peace to finish my work,' she addressed the clump of harebells. They nodded gently in the breeze, as if agreeing with her, and she started to sketch. But although she had no trouble concentrating before, this time her pencil refused to do as she wished, and twice she scored through the lines she had done, impatiently.

'If I was using my own pencil, it wouldn't have happened,' she blamed her tool unjustly, and for the umpteenth time her eyes strayed from her drawing, magnetised against her will by the tall, dark figure standing near the rocky outcrop. By just being there he destroyed her powers of concentration, and she glowered at him resentfully.

'I'll try shading instead, it might look better.' But although she resolutely tried to ignore Reeve and concentrate solely on her work, the figure that broke the skyline drew her eyes against her inclinations, until eventually her pencil slowed to a halt, and she scowled critically at the results of her efforts.

'It looks like a schoolchild doing art for 'O' levels,' she muttered disgustedly, and thrust the sketchblock back into the waterproof cover with a gesture of despair. She should have refused Reeve's company, even at the risk of upsetting her uncle, she might have known it would be useless to try and work while he was there.

'I'll finish the map, and then go straight back home,' she decided, and with a quick thrust of hands on knees she got to her feet quickly, before she could change her mind. Or before her courage failed her? Reeve's back looked uncomfortably square and unapproachable, and her resolve wavered as she got nearer to him. She wished he would turn round and speak, or at least give some sign that he was aware she was close behind him, but he seemed completely absorbed in the map, and she hesitated, undecided what to do next. What if he refused to give the map back to her? She could not use force to retrieve it. Her own slight figure against Reeve's infinitely superior height left her in no doubt on that score.

'I think your uncle's right, the line of the road does go to the right of the outcrop of rock, not to the left.'

He spoke over his shoulder, without bothering to look at her, and Marion started guiltily, as if she had been caught trying to creep up on him unawares. She resented the feeling. It was Reeve who was guilty, of ruining her sketching trip.

'I'll walk up to the ridge, it's easier to see from there,' she answered him noncommittally. His extra inches made it easy for him to see the line of the ancient roadway, but Marion needed the rise of the hill to give her enough height to make an accurate assessment. It was humiliating, but there was nothing she could do about it. She shrugged and turned away, biting her lip, and his voice checked her.

'You'll need the map to guide you.'

It was so easy. He simply reached out a long arm, and gave her the map. She did not have to demand it from him. She took it with disbelieving fingers. And then she looked up, and saw the half smile on his face, and her own flamed. He was indulging her, knowing she wanted the map. Divining her tension, and uncertainty, and determination to get the map back from him at all costs, and not knowing how. . . . So he gave it to her. Just like that. And his smile derided her.

She snatched the parchment from his hand, fighting down an almost uncontrollable impulse to throw it straight back in his face. Pure fury flooded through her, and left her bereft of speech. She turned on her heel abruptly, away from him, hiding her face. The quicker she decided where the road really did run, the better, then she could go back home, and Reeve—she gritted her teeth, and increased her pace—Reeve could stay up on the tops all day if he liked. For ever, for all she cared.

'The map was right in the first place.' She paused on the watershed and managed to find her voice. 'The line of the road goes to the left of the rocks.' She hardly gave the rocky outcrop and its surroundings a glance. It was only a matter of a few yards difference in any case, and at the moment she did not care if it was a couple of miles. The only thing that mattered was to get away—as far away as possible—from Reeve. His nearness had a devastating effect on her poise, and no amount of self-scorn, she discovered, made any difference. His presence—or could it be the memory of his kiss?—aroused longings she had never experienced before. And did not want to now, she told herself angrily. They did not enter into the scheme of things she had planned for her own future. Reeve did not enter. . . .

'The road goes to the right of the rock,' he contradicted her flatly. 'Look along the line of it, back there across the shoulder of the hill. It's obvious.'

'It's nothing of the kind,' she argued stubbornly, and ignored his pointing finger, refusing to look. Refusing to acknowledge that there was a line there at all, that could have indicated a road. 'Who in their right senses would climb above a rock outcrop, let alone drive cattle above it, when they could take the easy way along the downhill slope?'

'The drovers would,' he stated brusquely. 'They'd drive their animals higher rather than take them downwards on to the lip of an incline as steep as this one, and perhaps risk losing one of them if it slipped. You've only got to look,' he insisted, 'the line of the road is clear enough from here.'

'I've seen all I want to see,' she snapped back. 'That line to the right of the rock is nothing more than an old sheep-track.'

'Because the sheep take naturally to the safest way round the rocks, exactly the same as the old-time drovers would,' he retorted angrily. 'The line to the left of the rock is only an exposed stratum showing through, any amateur geologist would tell you that.'

'I'm no geologist, and it isn't clear to me.'

'Then compare it with the map.' He reached out impatiently to take it, and she jerked it out of his reach and let go of the end, allowing it to roll up tightly in her fingers.

'I don't need to,' she told him evenly. 'I've seen all that's necessary, and I'm going home.'

'Do you mean to say you've dragged me all the way up here, just for this?' Reeve rounded on her incredulously. 'What about your sketch, that you were so keen to finish?'

'I've done all I can to the sketch of the harebells,' she threw back, 'and as for my drawing of the hare, it's unlikely the animal will come within a mile of here with you tramping around. And I didn't drag you up here,' she reminded him tartly, 'I didn't even invite you.'

She turned away from him angrily, and in her haste she did not see the heather root. It lay gnarled and grey, like a snare to trap unwary feet, and it caught the toe of her shoe as she turned downhill. With a startled cry she flung up her arms in a vain bid to save herself from falling. The map flew from her hand in one direction, and the waterproof cover containing her sketchblock went in the other, and she twisted her face frantically to one side as the inhospitable top of a gorse bush reached up spiky fingers toward her cheeks.

'For two pins, I'd leave you to pick yourself off the prickles.'

Within an ace of the topmost spikes, Reeve grasped her and pulled her upright. With an effortless lift he pulled her over the gorse bush and stood her on her feet in front of him, and looked down at her with a mixture of anger and impatience.

'If you insist on blundering downhill without looking where you're going, at least find a softer spot to land on,' he told her harshly.

'My hairband slipped. I couldn't see—my hair got in my eyes——' She stammered to a confused halt. She dared not look up at him. Why did he have to hold on to her like that? Did he not know that his touch banked smouldering fires inside her that she had to quench now, while she still had the willpower, for fear they might ignite and engulf her. It would have been better, she thought desperately, if he had carried out his threat, and allowed her to fall. The gorse spikes were cruel, and her face might have been marked if he had not been there to save her, but the scars would have been nothing to the scars that his touch was engraving on her heart now.

'If that wretched hairband slips, it's not much use to you anyway, so why wear it?' he said impatiently. He raised his hand, and with a quick movement he slipped it free from her head, and as his fingers touched her hair his voice softened, unexpectedly. 'There ought to be a law against confining hair like this.' He ran long brown hands across the shining, honey-gold strands, stroking it away from her face, letting it slide through his fingers until it floated free in the breeze across her shoulders. 'It wants to be free.' He held it lightly, fingering it, and Marion quivered under his touch.

'So do I,' she choked. She tried to pull away from him, frightened of the fires that were kindled by his touch; frightened that he might sense them. But she could not move. Like the hare crouching before the approaching shadow of the helicopter, she was rooted to the ground.

'Do you, Marion?' he questioned softly, his eyes raking her face. 'I wonder.' She felt his lips touch the top of her head, and raised her eyes to his, mutely beseeching. Begging him for what? She hardly dared to think, To ask him to stop—or go on? While Reeve held her in his arms, pride left her, and she had no will of her own. He took her raised face as an invitation, and his lips stroked her forehead, moved down across the tip of her nose to the soft, tremulous corners of her mouth. She tried to draw back, to resist the consuming fire of her own feelings, but it was like trying to stem the tide. His lips hardened, feeling her response, and became demanding, possessive. 'Do you, Marion?' he repeated.

She could not answer him. His lips pressed hard against her own, denying her the ability to reply even if she knew what her answer would be. From somewhere far off, a dog barked, herding sheep, the calls of the flock came faintly to her ears like some low-played symphony in the background, with a deep overtone from the drone of an approaching plane. Or a helicopter?

'I'd forgotten Willy.' Reeve drew back first and looked down at her, and quick amusement lit his face. 'There's no privacy, even up here,' he grumbled, and bent to pick up her sketchblock.

'Stay close to me on the way down, it's steep.' He kept the sketchblock in his hands until they neared the Fleece, but he gave it to her then without demur, and they were in the house, and Marion had retreated to the kitchen quarters to find Mrs Pugh before she realised he had not also given her the map, which he retrieved at the same time as he picked up her sketchblock, and which he still retained, neatly rolled, in his own hands.

CHAPTER SIX

SHE hurried back to the hall.

'I'll take the map back to Uncle Miles.' With a set face she held out her hand for it, but this time he did not release it to her as he had done on the hill.

'I'll give it to him myself. I want to discuss where the road should go.'

'Where it's marked now,' she insisted, 'to the left of the rock outcrop.'

'No, it goes to the right, above the rocks.'

'Well now, I hoped you two might reach agreement on that, and settle the matter for me,' her uncle said mildly, coming through the door.

'I'm sure it's to the right of the rocks,' Reeve began, and Marion interrupted him angrily.

'That track's nothing but an old sheep walk, the line to the left of the rocks is clearly the road.'

'The line to the left of the rocks is clearly a stratum of rock exposed by the weather,' Reeve said coldly, almost, she thought furiously, as if he was talking to a particularly obtuse student.

'That's the difficulty with this sort of work,' Miles Dorman observed in his gentle voice, 'there are so many controversial points.'

'There's an easy way to settle this one,' Reeve spoke directly to her uncle and ignored Marion, 'come up with Willy and me in the helicopter tomorrow, and decide for yourself. The line of the road is clear enough on the hill.'

'It isn't clear to me. . . .'

But Reeve ignored her, and went on as if she had not spoken.

'It's even clearer from the air, you'll know then that the road lies. . . .'

'To the left of the rock,' Marion butted in triumphantly.

'To the right of the rock,' he finished adamantly. 'There's almost a precedent in another similar track north of the Pennines. It's mentioned in one of the reference books I've got at home. I've sent for it, so that you can see for yourself. That was one of the letters I posted this morning.' He addressed Marion now, and the steely look in his eyes told her that he knew that she had tried to read the addresses on the envelopes he pushed across the Post Office counter, and had deliberately put them so that the writing was the wrong way round for her to read, in order to foil her intention.

Her colour rose. She had never done such a thing before, prying was alien to her nature, but she squashed her conscience ruthlessly. If Reeve persisted in behaving in a mysterious manner, he must expect to invoke curiosity, she told herself resolutely, and ignored the small voice inside her which said that the business of the guests who came to stay at the Fleece was no concern of the proprietor or his family.

'I'll look forward to reading your book,' her uncle's gentle voice brought her back to her surroundings. 'It'll make an interesting comparison with the road here.' He was completely taken up with the world of the book he was writing, and remained blissfully ignorant of the antagonism its subject had caused between his niece and the guest, and Marion gave a gesture of impatience.

'I'm going to the stable,' she announced shortly. The block of stables at the rear of the hotel had been converted into garages, and a studio for herself in which the barman had erected a bench for her, which enabled her to leave her woodcut and tools undisturbed when she was not working there. They offered a haven now, and she took it. She had the greatest difficulty to restrain herself from running out of the room, but she managed to make a dignified exit, and reached the stable block with a sigh of relief. She could forget Reeve, and the road, and everything else while she was here.

Her woodcut was propped up on the bench facing the windows, which had been considerably enlarged in order to give her adequate light. She pulled away the covering cloth, and felt the tension ease from her as she looked at the long, narrow panel, one of a set of six, and already half carved. Her glance was critical, seeking faults that no other eyes would see, and her concentration acted like a door to shut out the world outside. Reeve, and the drovers' road, and the petty irritations that seemed an inevitable part of their everyday contact with one another, receded from her mind. She put down the waterproof cover containing her sketchblock, and drew out the work she had been engaged on that morning. Most of it was scored over, but what she had drawn previously remained untouched, and a small, satisfied sigh escaped her.

'This will just finish off the corner,' she murmured to herself. 'The hare can go further along the panel.'

It already held an intricately carved selection of animals and birds, set among their natural habitat, and captured in mid-movement with an almost uncanny lifelikeness that made the carved creatures seem to the casual observer merely to have paused to gaze back for a moment at the looker on, before resuming whatever activity it was they were engaged upon when interrupted. It was this ability to capture the spirit of pulsing life in her carvings that stamped Marion's work as peculiarly her own, and made it in universal demand, and was the result of long hours of patient observation, and a deep knowledge and love of her subjects. She reached for her chisel.

'I think I'll round off this leaf a bit more, it's too sharp for a cowslip.' She set to work taking wafer-thin shavings from the leaf until she was absolutely satisfied as to its shape. She stepped back to get it into better perspective. 'A bit more off this side, and it'll be just right.' Her chisel poised, she began to apply pressure.

'So this is where you work.'

She spun round. The chisel flew from her nerveless fingers, but the pressure she had begun to apply to the handle took its toll, and the razor-keen blade caught her wrist as it fell.

'You again!'

The tool clattered noisily on to the quarry floor, and blood welled from a diagonal gash across her wrist. Reeve stepped forward quickly.

'Never mind that.' She tried to pull her hand away.

'Don't be silly,' he said abruptly, and caught her firmly to him. 'Sit down,' he ordered, and pulled a nearby wooden

stool towards her with a deft kick of his foot. 'Let me see
how bad it is.'

Marion sat down suddenly, and let him see. Without
warning she began to feel distinctly odd. She tried to tell
herself that it was the cut, but the sight of blood had never
affected her before. She refused to acknowledge that it
could be the feel of Reeve's fingers on her wrist, his other
hand on her shoulder, holding her against him lest she
should fall. The stable walls seemed to be trying to per-
form some sort of dance. Vaguely she could feel Reeve
doing something to her wrist with what felt like a piece
of soft cloth. He tipped her face upwards towards him, with
his fingers under her chin, and she gave a murmur of protest, but he ignored it and propped his foot on the bars
of the stool to make a back for her with his knee.

'You're as white as a ghost. Lean against me,' he commanded her.

She closed her eyes and did as she was told. The stool
had no back to it, and she had to lean against something
or topple over. His knee dug into her spine and she moved
restlessly, seeking a more comfortable position. He stopped whatever he was doing with the cloth, and pulled her
more firmly against him.

'Is that better?'

She nodded wordlessly. The faint spicy tang of expensive
after-shave lotion permeated her consciousness.

He doesn't smoke. The thought crossed her mind,
vaguely noticing. She did not like the smell of smoke. It
clung to her clothes and hair and skin with a rank, all per-
vading odour that offended Marion's fastidious nostrils.

'No, I don't smoke. Why?'

She did not realise she had spoken aloud. She opened
her eyes. The walls of the stable obligingly resumed their
solid stance.

'Did you want a cigarette?' Reeve persisted.

'No, I don't either. Smoke, I mean.' She felt his voice
vibrate through his chest under the softness of his sweater,
and it dawned on her that the reason the vibration came

through so clearly was because her right ear was leaning against the sweater in question. She sat up abruptly, her former pallor giving way to a rising tide of pink.

'Don't stand up suddenly,' he warned her quickly, 'you might keel over.'

'I'm all right now.' She had to get up—quickly. Whatever he said. Sitting on the stool, with his knee at her back, and her head leaning against his shoulder, with his one arm round her and his hands tending her injured wrist, was creating more chaos with her circulation than the cut itself. Her heart beat rapidly, making up for its dereliction of a moment ago, and although the stable walls stayed still she felt dizzy, and she felt herself sway.

'I told you not to stand up suddenly,' he said sharply, and put out his hand to steady her.

'I said I'm fine.' She resented Reeve ordering her about, and showed it. Why did she have to feel faint now? she wondered desperately. With a supreme effort she pulled her reeling senses together and moved out of reach of his hand. She had never fainted in her life before, and she had to choose a time when Reeve was around to disgrace herself, she poured silent scorn on her weakness. The fact that Reeve was there in the first place was the sole reason she had cut herself. Remembering it goaded her to anger.

'If you hadn't come creeping up behind me like that, I shouldn't have cut myself,' she accused him. She inspected her wrist. It was swathed in soft lawn, its erstwhile snowy whiteness dotted here and there with dark smudges that —she narrowed her eyes and watched them keenly—did not seem to be getting any bigger, so it must have stopped bleeding, thanks to Reeve's prompt first aid.

'I didn't creep up behind you,' he denied, 'you were so engrossed in your work that you didn't hear me come in.'

'You shouldn't have come to this part of the stable block at all,' she threw back at him, 'the garages are clearly marked at the other end of the yard.'

'I didn't come to get the car.' He eyed her coldly, stung by her tone. 'I came to give you this—though I wish now I hadn't bothered,' he added bitingly, and held out her hairband towards her.

'I thought you said I shouldn't wear it.' She eyed it with disfavour. This was the third time he had given it back to her.

'No more you should,' he stated flatly, 'but it's your property. I don't purloin other people's belongings. Besides, a hairband wouldn't be of much use to me.' His lips tilted slightly, and Marion's tightened.

'In that case I'll relieve you of it,' she said sarcastically, and grasped at the length of brown velvet ribbon with impatient fingers. Her haste was her undoing. She turned away before Reeve could loosen it, and she felt a tug. She turned back with a frown.

'It's caught on my finger. Wait a minute, while I loose it.' The elastic part of it had twisted round his finger and tightened at her pull, and he proceeded to remove it with a lack of haste that flooded Marion with impatient irritation. She did not know whether to continue to hold her side of it, or release and risk it dropping to the floor when he freed himself. She felt like a puppy caught on the end of a lead. The thought annoyed her irrationally, and she gave the velvet band a tug.

'Now you've tightened it again,' he observed, and started to unloosen it again with maddening deliberation.

'I can't stay here all day.'

'There's no need for you to.' He released it at last, and the elastic shot back with a sharp flick against Marion's fingers. It did not hurt her, but the suddenness of it made her jump, and the ghost of a grin turned the corners of Reeve's lips upwards.

'That wasn't funny,' she snapped, and thrust the hairband angrily into her slacks pocket. Without waiting to see if he would come out of the stable with her, she turned on her heel and hurried towards the kitchen quarters on the other side of the yard. He would not follow her through

into the domestic quarters, she felt sure. Or did she? Reeve
had a disconcerting habit of doing the unexpected.

She risked a glance over her shoulder as she turned the
handle of the kitchen door, but he was nowhere in sight.
She hesitated, uncertain whether to carry on indoors or
to go back. Why hadn't he followed her out of the stable?
Perhaps he had remained to look at her woodcut. He might
conceivably be interested. She shrugged. Doubtless he was
finding fault with that, as well. She turned indoors.

'Is that you, Marion?'

'Yes. I'm just going upstairs for something, then I'm
off back to the stable.' With typical lack of pride it did
not occur to Marion to relegate her transformed workroom
to the status of a studio.

'I'll call you when it's time for lunch.'

Marion breathed a sigh of relief that the housekeeper
had no opportunity to see her swathed wrist. Mrs Pugh
had more than once voiced her unease at the razor-sharp
tools she used, and she did not feel she could cope with
another argument on the subject now. She reached her
room and sank thankfully on to the side of her bed, until
she realised she had her hairband in her hand. With a
grimace she got to her feet and pulled open one of her
dressing table drawers. With a gesture of rejection she
flung the hairband to the back of the drawer and slammed
it shut with a decisive bang.

'I don't want to see the wretched thing ever again,' she
muttered, and wondered as she said it whether she meant
the hairband or Reeve. The thought of him brought her
attention back to her wrist. She unwrapped his handkerchief gingerly, and gave a small puff of relief as she surveyed the cut. It was a long one, but it was not deep, she
saw gratefully. Her hands were a precious asset, and the
thought of an injury that might put her fingers out of
action turned her cold with dread.

'A plaster will be enough for this,' she told herself,
and turned once again to her dressing table. The drawer
that now housed her hairband produced the required

first aid, and she smoothed an unobtrusive dressing over the evidence of her accident.

'I'll soak this hanky in cold water, it's a shame to stain it.' She seemed to be making a habit of washing out things for Reeve, she thought impatiently, noting the neatly monogrammed initials in a corner of the fine lawn. R. H. intertwined, and beautifully worked. First it was his duster, and now his handkerchief.

'Have you cut yourself, Miss Marion? Is it bad?' A homely country voice interrupted her, and an equally homely face appeared round the door, and Marion summoned up a smile at the sight of their daily help.

'Sssh, not so loud!' she warned. 'It's only a scratch really, but you know how nervous Mrs Pugh is of my chisels.'

'She does go on a bit,' the newcomer agreed cheerfully. 'It's bad enough to stain your hanky, though,' she eyed the contents of the washbasin with a perceptive glance.

'It's Mr Harland's hanky.' She could not hide its size. Rose had keen eyes, and would instantly put the wrong conclusion on her action if she tried to cover up what she was doing. 'He saw the chisel fly, and came across to find out what damage I'd done.'

'Ah well, it's lucky it was no worse,' Rose said philosophically, her curiosity satisfied. 'Let me take the hanky downstairs with me, I've got some towels to iron for Mrs Pugh, and I can iron the hanky at the same time.'

'That's kind of you.' Marion wrung it out and handed it over without regret. Rose could iron it, and she could also give it back to Reeve, and no doubt he would say thank you—properly—to Rose if he wanted to, she added to herself witheringly.

'Oh, by the way, miss,' Rose halted on her way to the door, 'I've put a bundle of papers on your chair—the one by your bed,' and she pointed.

'Not more betting slips found behind the bar?' Marion smiled.

'Not this time.' Rose did not return her smile, in fact she

looked troubled. 'These papers were in Mr Harland's room, in one of those plastic folder things like they use in offices. It was on his dressing table, and I picked it up to dust underneath, and all the papers slipped out. Them plastic things are that slippy, the papers shot all over the place, and I don't know which one's which to put them back again,' she finished worriedly.

'I'll sort them out for you, and return them to Mr Harland.' Marion owed her that for ironing the handkerchief.

'He might wonder where they've got to if he comes up to his room,' the file of papers was obviously worrying the daily help.

'I'll see to them right away,' Marion promised, and reaching over she picked them up from the chair. 'No wonder you dropped them.' She gave an exclamation of annoyance as she grasped the end of the dark blue, opaque plastic folder, and the sheaf of papers it contained suddenly hurtled out of it without warning, and scattered across the carpet. 'This folder is as slippery as if it's been greased!' She bent to pick up the closely written sheets, and spread them out on her bed.

'I'll go and do Mrs Pugh's ironing, and bring this hanky back in a while.' Rose left her to the incomprehensible task of file sorting in favour of more familiar ground, and Marion bent her attention to her self-imposed chore.

'It's a good job the pages are numbered,' she muttered thankfully. It was not a particularly onerous task. There were about twenty-five sheets in all—no, twenty-six. She pulled what seemed to be the end sheet out of the pile triumphantly. It was signed and dated. She glanced at the signatures. There were two. One, in a spidery sort of script, said 'William Mills.' So that was Willy's other name. Marion smiled. She had not caught it when they were first introduced, and did not bother to look in the hotel register afterwards. 'Willy' seemed appropriate enough on its own for the friendly little pilot.

The other signature belonged to Reeve. Although the

sheets she was handling were merely a carbon copy of an original, probably the one he had posted that morning, the bold, clear strokes of his name stood out, indicative of the confident, decisive nature of the writer. The whole report seemed to be in Reeve's writing. She riffled through the pages.

'Oh no, there's an attachment.' There were only about five pages written in Willy's spidery hand; the rest had been done by Reeve himself. Probably after he left her the evening before, after he had kissed her. She scowled at the offending pages. It showed how casual his caress had been, that he could dismiss it so lightly in order to concentrate on a complicated report such as this. She closed her mind to the sleepless night she herself had endured as a result of his kisses, and the feelings they had aroused in her, and forced her attention back to the papers.

There were sketches and tables of figures among them that looked as if they might be the results of a geological survey. Perhaps, after all, the report had nothing to do with his work, whatever that might be. Perhaps Reeve was compiling a book or something of the same nature as her uncle—their interests seemed to run parallel. She looked at the papers with keener attention. The top page still lay on the counterpane, and she picked it up and tapped the bundle into a neat pile between her fingers. The paper clip that originally held them was caught on the top of the folder, which was probably why they had come apart and slipped out in the first place. She retrieved it and gripped the bundle securely together again, smoothing it flat with her hand. Her finger traced the underlining of the title—a single, thick black stroke, drawn by a writer who was in no doubt of what he wanted to say. But it was the wording of the title that arrested her attention.

'Fallbeck Valley Dam Project.'

The letters seemed to leap out at her from the whiteness of the page, and she stared at them in stunned bewilderment. What did it mean—dam project? Dams were things made to hold back water. They had nothing to do with ancient roads. And who would want to build a dam in Fallbeck Valley? The only waterway there was the beck. Its name belied its size, it was in fact a deep and fast moving stream, fed by the copious waterfall that hurtled over Fallbeck Scar, whose rocky fastnesses hid the spring that gave the waterway its birth.

People only built dams across waterways like the beck when they wanted to flood some valley or other to make a.... Marion could not bring herself to even think of the word. A cold sense of dread gripped her with icy fingers, and the first lines of writing underneath the title drew her eyes with an evil fascination. They said, unequivocally, in coldly unemotional business phrasing,

'Fallbeck Valley is considered to be an ideal site for a reservoir of sufficient capacity to supply the city of —— with its total domestic requirement of water, thus enabling the capacity of the present reservoir sited to the south of the city to be concentrated on its growing industrial requirements. There appear to be no insuperable obstacles to the implementation of this plan....'

She read no further. As the implication of what she was looking at penetrated her consciousness, hot rage flooded through her mind. So this was why Reeve had come to the valley! Curiously she did not include Willy in her condemnation. Willy was merely the pilot, doing as he was told —doing what Reeve told him. And Reeve had come to turn the valley—their valley—into a reservoir. To dispossess its people of their homes, their land, their livelihood, and drown Fallbeck village, and the familiar steeply-sided vale under immeasurable gallons of water. She gazed through a mist at the papers she had clipped together so carefully, and they shook in her fingers as she held them.

'Do you usually sneak into your guests' rooms and purloin their private correspondence? Or is this because you couldn't satisfy your curiosity this morning, and read the addresses on the envelopes I put on the Post Office counter?'

Reeve's voice was as cold as his eyes, and they looked

at her from the open doorway, grey as slate, and just about as hard. She had not heard him come. Her mind only registered the fact that he was there. That he was responsible....

'This is why you asked me all those questions this morning.'

She rose slowly to her feet, ignoring his remark. Ignoring the anger on his face. What did it matter how his papers had come into her possession? Her sense of outrage was such that she did not care what he thought of her. It did not occur to her to even try to explain. Last night, and again this morning, she had responded to his kisses, returned them with an ardour that equalled his own. She burned with shame at the memory.

'When the postmistress said her licence might not be renewed, you told her maybe it wouldn't happen.' Her voice came out hoarse, strained with loathing and disbelief. 'And all the time you knew,' she accused him. She held out the folder of papers towards him, noted dispassionately that the end of the plastic folder shook, responding to the violent trembling that possessed her hands.

'All the time you intended it to happen,' she whispered.

The thought of the questions he had asked her, and worse, the answers she had given to him, appalled her. She had told him, in as many words, that the school stood in imminent danger of closing through lack of pupils. And the church was—how had she put it? 'Architecturally uninteresting'. From which he would infer that no one would fight to save the building on the grounds of historical importance. She had even—Marion blanched at the memory— she had even suggested to him when they were at the airport together that her uncle took little interest in running the hotel, since he became a widower. If Reeve had his way, Zilla Wade's prophecy that the Fleece would be the next to lose its licence might become even more true than the farmer's wife bargained for.

'You—traitor!' she ground the words through set teeth.

'Traitor?' His eyebrows arched. 'Might I ask to whom?'

he enquired of her icily. 'I owe no allegiance to Fallbeck. Only to my firm.'

'I've ironed the hanky for you, Miss Marion.'

Neither of them heard Rose; they were too absorbed in one another. They did not see her outstretched hand, offering back the neatly ironed and folded square of lawn, and when neither of them offered to take it, place it on the table behind the door and tiptoe silently away.

'I suppose you think loyalty to your firm gives you the right to turn the inhabitants of an entire valley out of their homes, in order to flood it to make your wretched reservoir,' she cried angrily.

'The people will be generously compensated,' he began, and she interrupted him furiously.

'Compensated? What with—money?' She laughed without humour. 'I suppose you think money is adequate compensation for losing your home, your land. . . .'

'The plan is only at the recommendation stage as yet.'

'And you've recommended it,' she cried bitterly. 'Don't try to deny it. It says so here.' She thrust the folder of papers towards him. 'And you've also said,' she read his own words back to him with bitter inflection, 'you've also said "there appear to be no insuperable obstacles." ' Her chin rose defiantly. 'That's just where you're mistaken,' she assured him grimly. 'You're looking at one insuperable obstacle right now! Here, have back your report—recommendation—whatever you call it!' She flung the folder haphazardly in his general direction, not caring whether he caught it or not. Let him have the job of putting the papers back together again! she thought angrily. He caught the folder, but only just, and by dint of stepping backwards out of her doorway on to the landing, but he managed to field it, though his head came up angrily, and he made as if to speak, but she did not give him the opportunity.

'I'll put a stop to your infamous plan if it's the last thing I do!' she vowed. And before he had a chance to answer her, she slammed her bedroom door in his face.

CHAPTER SEVEN

'HE pretended to be sympathetic to the postmistress, and
all the time he knew!' Marion exclaimed passionately. A
thought struck her, and she added consideringly, 'he was
probably behind the decision of the Post Office not to
renew the licence, if they were aware what his intentions
are with regard to the valley.' She thrust her bowl of soup
away from her untouched, and leaned her arms on the table.
The bowl and its liquid reminded her sickeningly of a
reservoir.

'Are you sure of this, Marion?' Her uncle looked across
from the other side of the table, for once, she saw with
relief, shaken out of himself sufficiently to take an interest
in the present, rather than in history.

'I read it myself in a report Reeve wrote last night.' She
explained how she came to have the report in her possession. 'He didn't deny it, so it must be true,' she said stormily.

'That means everyone in Fallbeck will be affected.' Miles
Dorman looked troubled.

'Of course they will.' Marion leaned forward tensely. 'A
reservoir will take the whole valley. And there's another
thing,' she remembered, 'Zilla Wade was in the Post Office
when we went there this morning, and she said the Fleece
would probably be the next to lose its licence to trade.
Perhaps she's heard something we haven't?' she hazarded.
'You know how she loves to get hold of a titbit of gossip,
and use it to confound somebody. Have you heard anything
about your licence, Uncle Miles?' she asked anxiously. The
Fleece was his home as well as his livelihood, and although
he was close to pension age, it was unthinkable he should
be turned out of his home now.

'I've heard nothing at all about the licence for the
Fleece.' He spoke so decisively that she had to believe him,

but just the same she glanced towards Mrs Pugh silently seeking confirmation.

'Neither have I.' The housekeeper gave her a significant look, her straight gaze telling Marion more clearly than words that Mrs Pugh would have made it her business to find out if such knowledge had reached her uncle, and moreover do something about it. Marion relaxed slightly. Her uncle and the Fleece were safe in Mrs Pugh's hands. And she intended to see that they remained so, she vowed silently.

'If this plan goes through....' Miles Dorman began thoughtfully.

'It won't,' Marion declared heatedly.

'No, but just consider for a moment if it should,' he insisted in his gentle voice.

'It would mean turning everyone in the valley out of their homes,' Marion exploded wrathfully.

'It would mean that the contractors responsible for the project would be obliged to offer equivalent suitable accommodation elsewhere,' he pointed out. 'Just think what that would involve, for the firm concerned. The reservoir must be of considerable importance for them to even contemplate such a step, let alone get as far as a survey and recommendation.'

'It is important—desperately important. That's the reason I'm here.'

They all turned, startled, and Reeve shut the door quietly behind him, and advanced into the room.

'I didn't hear you knock,' Marion criticised sharply.

'I didn't,' he replied blandly. 'But I heard your voices raised in here, and I guessed what you were talking about. So I thought I'd join you. At least then you'd hear the— rest of the information,' he stressed 'rest of the information' with a cold glance at Marion, and she glared back at him, unabashed by his barb. 'You'd have the rest of the information straight from the horse's mouth, so to speak,' he finished.

'You'd better have your coffee with us,' Mrs Pugh invited noncommittally, 'then we can talk in comfort. We've finished our meal.' The guests ate first, so Reeve and Willy must have finished too.

'Why us? Why Fallbeck?' Marion burst out the moment Reeve sat down. She pushed her coffee to one side with the same distaste she accorded her soup. 'Why Fallbeck?' she repeated. 'Surely you could have found another site, somewhere else?'

'They all say that.'

Was there just the hint of weariness in Reeve's voice? If there was, Marion disregarded it with a shrug. If he went about building reservoirs and dispossessing people of their homes and land, he must expect to encounter opposition.

'It's always "Why me? Why not someone else?"' he went on. 'But people must have water. And to supply water on tap, there must be reservoirs. You were quick enough to side with the people who built the ancient roads, and point out the benefits they brought in their wake,' he reminded her remorselessly.

'That was different.'

'Only in principle, my dear,' Miles Dorman's voice brought Marion's attention away from Reeve with an astounded gasp.

'You're not on his side, surely?' A hot tide of indignation choked her words to an astonished halt, and she gestured towards Reeve as if she could not bear to even speak his name.

'I don't think it's a matter of taking sides,' her uncle said consideringly. 'There are bound to be fors and againsts in a scheme like this, but you must see that it'll have to be viewed impartially by whatever authority is responsible—weighing the eventual gain against the immediate loss.'

'I thought you might take that view,' Reeve murmured, and Marion remembered with an uneasy qualm that he had implied something of the sort when they were driving into Dale End together. 'Your uncle's research must make him appreciate the necessity for change,' he had said, and she wondered at the time why he said it. Now she

knew. He had read Miles Dorman's character with deadly
accuracy, she realised bitterly. That was the worst of
academics, they viewed everything as if it was already
history. Marion looked across at her uncle with affectionate exasperation. He would weigh up the pros and cons
like an outsider observing a play, and completely ignore
the disruption to their own and other people's lives. If
Fallbeck valley was flooded, the Fleece would be lost with
all the rest of the dwellings, and they themselves would
have to be transplanted to a new environment. That was
what Reeve must have meant when he commented on
Ben Wade's newly acquired sheep, and the noise they were
making. Another memory came to prick her, and she remembered uneasily her own explanation to Reeve.

'As soon as they get used to it, they'll settle down.
Sheep are like that.'

And his reply, that even at the time she thought odd.

'So are people.'

'The immediate loss will be our homes,' Marion burst
out, 'and so far as any gain is concerned, you'll simply be
taking more water to a city that already has a reservoir,
according to your report.'

'But an inadequate one,' Reeve pointed out.

'Then enlarge it.'

'That's impossible.'

'How do you know?'

'Because I've already explored that route,' he retorted,
his curt tone indicative of tightly controlled patience.
'Believe me, we're only considering Fallbeck valley as a
very last resort.'

'Why should I believe you?' Marion threw back at him
witheringly. 'You came here under false pretences....'

'I came here under no pretence at all.' The semblance
of patience vanished, and his voice hardened perceptibly.
'Willy and I booked in as paying guests at the Fleece, with
the same right as everyone else to privacy as to the reason
for our visit. Why we came here is no concern of yours.'
His voice held the same steely quality as his eyes.

'How can you stand there and say it's not our concern, when it involves our property, the very houses we live in,' Marion rounded on him incredulously. 'If it's not our concern, whose is it?' she cried.

'No one's as yet,' he answered her sharply. 'I've told you, the whole thing is still only at the exploratory stage. All my report contains is a recommendation, nothing more. And because of that,' he turned to Miles Dorman as if seeking the help of a more reasonable intelligence, and Marion's lips tightened ominously, 'because of that I must ask you to keep what you know—what you've discovered,' he threw the words at her accusingly, with a contempt that made her flinch, and then her chin rose. The report had come into her possession purely by chance, Reeve could think what he liked, she thought defiantly. If he chose to believe she stole it, that was his affair. That, at least, was no concern of hers.

'I must insist that you keep what you've learned strictly to yourselves,' he finished, and his voice bit like an east wind. 'There's no point in creating unnecessary alarm among the inhabitants of the valley, when it's possible that my recommendation may be turned down.'

'I think he's right to ask that of us, Marion,' Miles Dorman said seriously, and she shrugged.

'Oh, very well, if you say so,' she conceded, 'but only because you say so.' She would not have Reeve think she was doing it because he commanded her. 'And by the time your precious recommendation is accepted, as you know it will be, it'll be too late then for anybody to do anything about it,' she sneered.

'Nonsense!' Reeve said shortly. 'If my report is accepted as it stands, there'll have to be a public enquiry for all the people involved. All points of view have to be taken into consideration.'

'Whitewash!' Marion debunked his explanation with scant ceremony. 'When big business decides it wants something, what chance has an ordinary person got?'

'This isn't big business,' he contradicted her evenly.

'This is a public authority, which has an obligation to its ratepayers to provide them with an adequate supply of water. My firm is merely the one that has won the contract to give them what they require. We not only do the surveying and the building, we act as middlemen in the negotiations between the authority and the people involved, to come to an amicable agreement on matters of compensation and so on.'

'An amicable agreement?' Marion laughed without humour. 'And I suppose if the people in the valley don't agree, they'll have a compulsory purchase order made against them, and be paid minimum compensation. What choice have they got?' she exclaimed, and she did not know how near to despair her voice sounded.

'If it comes to a public enquiry, why not attend and find out?' he asked reasonably. 'And in the meantime,' his voice became brisk, 'none of us know what the outcome of my report will be, so the only thing to do is to try and forget it for now.' He dismissed the subject and turned to Miles Dorman. 'There was something else I came to see you about. Willy's going up in the 'copter this afternoon, I thought you might like to go with him while the weather holds good?'

'Indeed I would.' Her uncle accepted the offer with alacrity, and Marion stared at him in amazement. How could he even think of going up in the helicopter, now he knew what Reeve had come to the valley for? She herself could not bear to think of remaining in the same room with the man, let alone accept a trip in his wretched flying machine, she thought stormily. She opened her mouth to protest, then closed it again with a shrug of resignation. It was useless to try and make her uncle any different from what he was. The historian in him lay uppermost, and even now the drovers' road was of paramount importance in his mind, far exceeding the threat to his home and livelihood.

'I must see the ancient road just once more, while I still have the opportunity,' he muttered, 'before it's covered with water.' So he, too, accepted the reservoir as inevitable, she thought hopelessly.

'The water won't touch the drovers' road, that's on the other side of the watershed, and too high anyway,' Reeve put his mind at rest. 'The height of the reservoir will come to about half way up the hillside, no more.' He sounded as if he had already put an invisible Plimsoll line across the fellsides, she realised with dismay, although reason told her such a survey would have to be thorough, even to the smallest detail. And in spite of his assurances, she noticed Reeve spoke as if the reservoir was already an accomplished fact.

'I'll go and fetch my maps and fieldglasses.' Miles Dorman hurried out of the room.

'And I'll let Willy know you're going with him.' Reeve followed, and Marion moved disconsolately kitchenwards with Mrs Pugh.

'How can Uncle Miles bother about an old drovers' road at a time like this?' she began hotly.

'It's a bombshell, I'll admit,' Mrs Pugh replied cautiously, 'but like Mr Harland says, it's not much good getting upset about it until we know whether his recommendation is accepted, and there's something to get upset about,' she reasoned practically.

'But think of the consequences. . . .'

'I am thinking about them,' the older woman replied seriously, 'and I can best do that when I've got my kitchen to myself so I can finish off the rest of the ironing,' she added significantly.

Marion slipped reluctantly off the end of the table, and felt a soft touch on her knee. She looked down.

'I'll take Gyp for a walk,' she succumbed to the silent pleading of the elderly border collie. 'Come on, you haven't had a lot of exercise for a couple of days. We'll go as far as the waterfall over the Scar.' She did not know if Mrs Pugh heard her. The capable fingers were already smoothing a sleeve across the top of the ironing board, and reaching for the iron, trying it gingerly to see if it was hot enough. It was, and she bent her grey head over her task, as if removing creases from the freshly washed garment was the most important thing in the world. Marion gave her a puzzled look. She started to say something, and thought better of it. It seemed little use talking to a bent head, and she closed the door quietly behind her.

'What's the matter with them both?' she asked Gyp, letting her exasperation escape with a rush once she was outside. 'First Uncle Miles, then Mrs Pugh. They act as if the reservoir isn't going to happen!'

Her only reply was a waving plume, and Marion smiled and rubbed the silky head. 'I'm glad Uncle Miles had you,' she told him affectionately, and lengthened her stride to keep pace with the collie. Despite his ten years, he was remarkably active, his life of herding on the hill had given him a wiry agility that stretched even Marion's energy at the beginning of the walk.

'Try and remember you're retired,' she protested at last, and paused for breath at the stepping stones over the beck, where the path touched the edge of the Wade holding. Gyp danced easily across the wet slabs, surefooted, but Marion proceeded with more care. She did not want a wetting to cap the day, she decided ruefully, and paused for a moment to gaze down into the clear water. It would be icy cold, she knew without trying, fresh from who knew what depths in the timeless rocks of the Scar. And the beck was deep, too. No matter how hot the summer, the flow from the spring that fed it never slackened. When it was dammed, it would not take long to flood the valley.

'No!' She checked her thinking sharply. '*If* it's dammed.' Her chin set in a determined line.

'It's no good tha' looking for fish in the beck near the Scar. Water's too cold.'

She jerked upright and nearly lost her balance as a rough voice spoke from the bank behind her.

'Hello, Ben. You made me jump, I didn't hear you.' She saw vexedly from the grin on the youth's face that he had intended to startle her, and was enjoying her discomfiture.

No doubt he would have enjoyed it even more if she had lost her balance and received a ducking, she thought tartly. Ben Wade had inherited more than a little of his mother's malicious nature.

'Come on, Gyp. If we're going as far as the waterfall, we'll have to get on.' She did not feel in the mood to remain and talk with Ben, she still felt churned up inside herself from her clash with Reeve.

'It'd be better if your uncle had let that one be put down.' The youth gave Gyp a glowering look. For once he seemed inclined to linger and talk, she supposed it was too much to expect him to be amiable as well, Marion thought impatiently.

'Gyp is in perfectly good condition,' she answered firmly. 'He may be past working the hill, but he makes an excellent companion for my uncle.'

'Dogs is the same as folks,' Ben answered her dourly, 'when they've got nowt to do, they start looking for mischief. Mind you keep him away from the sheep. Herding ain't that different from harrying, an' he's as like to take to the one as he was to t'other,' he predicted darkly.

'Gyp's shown no sign of wanting to harry sheep,' Marion retorted sharply.

'See as he doan, not while he's by our flocks,' Ben warned her illhumouredly. 'Heel, you!' he growled an order to his own collie, which skulked behind him, a snarl lifting its lips as it passed close to Gyp. The latter replied in kind, and Marion moved quickly towards the opposite bank of the beck.

'Come!' Hurriedly she set Gyp moving ahead of her. Really, Ben was impossible! she thought angrily. And his dog was as bad. A fight between the two collies was more than she felt she could endure in her present state of mind. She glanced back over her shoulder, but man and dog were already some way off, and heading in the opposite direction.

'If it was only the Wade holding that was affected, I don't

think I'd put up any resistance to the reservoir,' she muttered crossly to herself.

She strode out behind Gyp, seeking relief in movement, but she could not outpace her own thoughts. What if Ben was right about the dog? she wondered uneasily. The possibility worried her more than she cared to admit. Miles Dorman had become fond of the dog, and she knew it was a concession by its master that had allowed it to live beyond its useful working span. Gyp came from the same farm as the sheep which Ben Wade had purchased. Its owner was selling up and moving out. Doubtless if he had remained to farm in the vicinity, self-interest in the form of concern for the safety of his own flocks, would have obliged him to follow the accepted norm and have the dog put down. Marion sighed. One problem seemed to pile on top of another, and there did not appear to be a ready solution to any of them.

She heard the engine of the helicopter just before she reached the waterfall. She turned to pinpoint it against the blue of the sky. It was following its original route through the gap in the hills at the other end of Merevale, and tracing the line of the ridge dividing the two valleys. She quickened her pace. If she could gain the waterfall in time, she could climb up among its rocks and watch the activities of the helicopter while remaining unobserved herself. She saw the machine pause over where the rocky outcrop lay, probably to enable Miles Dorman to study more closely the controversial section of the drovers' road.

'I hope he finds it goes to the left of the rocks,' she wished fervently. 'He must find it goes to the left of the rocks. . . .' It was unthinkable that it should be otherwise after the stand she had taken against Reeve. She closed her mind resolutely to any possibility of Reeve being in the right, and continued doggedly upwards. Gyp went on ahead, as surefooted as a mountain goat. Once he disturbed a huddle of sheep from behind a rock. They jumped up, protesting, and Marion caught her breath sharply, but the dog ignored them and continued on its course, and she relaxed again.

'I'm just being silly,' she scolded herself. But she knew there was logic behind Ben's warning, and she confessed it had made her nervous, as he no doubt meant it to. She thrust the thought of Ben from her mind and concentrated on climbing high enough to see both the valleys. From such a vantage point she could watch every move the helicopter made, and remain invisible herself.

Gyp found a spot for her. He stopped and waited for her to catch up, and when she joined him she saw just ahead of them a patch of green turf at the bottom of a smooth slab of rock, out of the way of the spray from the waterfall. It was not unlike the spot from which she had done her sketching, further along the ridge, and it looked cool and inviting after her long climb.

'This is as far as I go,' she told the dog, and sank down thankfully. Gyp did the same, as glad to rest as she, and a wave of relief passed over her as he settled unbidden at her feet.

'This is ridiculous,' she told herself. If she was not careful she would find herself watching every move Gyp made, from now on. But wasn't that what Ben intended? She leaned back against the rock, willing herself to relax. The sound of the waterfall blotted out the drone of the helicopter, and imperceptibly her tension lessened. The soothing roar of the fall had a soporific effect, and it gradually quietened the turmoil in her mind until Reeve and Ben and the helicopter became things apart, for the moment anyway of less importance. She watched the machine lazily. One part of her noticed that the shadow lay behind it. It was later in the day than the first time she saw it across the fellside, and the sun was in a different position, throwing the darkness on its other side.

She wondered if the hare was there, perhaps come back again to feed, and even now crouching, fearful of the shadow. The helicopter did not seem to be hovering quite so low this time, and because of this the shade it cast was not so black, but it was still there, symptomatic of the shadow that hovered over the whole valley. She could imagine Reeve in the cabin of the machine, looking down, his hawk face intent, his eyes on his prey. For surely, she thought passionately, that this was what the valley was, to him? And he was waiting, biding his time until he stooped, as an eagle would stoop, to grasp his chosen with the concrete talons of his dam.

She shivered, and felt cravenly glad that the shadow, this time, came nowhere near to where she sat. And then—quite suddenly—it did. But it was not cast by the helicopter. Black and menacing, a long bar of darkness strode without warning straight across the grassy spot where she sat. It blotted out the sunshine, and seemed infinitely darker than the shade from the helicopter. It was totally unexpected, and to Marion's startled senses it seemed inexplicably threatening. The shadow of an eagle.... She sat up abruptly, and instinct guided her eyes to seek the sky. They met instead the dark, aquiline visage of Reeve, standing behind her. His face was impassive, his grey eyes half hooded, and he watched her without speaking. How long had he been standing there? She had no means of knowing. He must have moved, for his shadow to fall across her. A thrill of something like fear shot through her, as it had on the day she watched the hare. And as on that day, anger followed the fear.

'I thought you were in the helicopter with Willy.' She said the first thing that came into her head.

'I said Willy was taking the 'copter up. I didn't say anything about going with him myself.'

He was splitting hairs, and she gave him an angry glare. He had not said anything about following her up the hillside, either.

'Why didn't you speak, instead of creeping up behind me like that?' she snapped, and jumped to her feet. She felt at a disadvantage, looking up at him.

'You sat so still I thought you'd gone to sleep. And Gyp didn't stir either.' He reached down and rubbed the dog's head, and was rewarded by a waving tail.

'He's glad to rest when he's come this far,' she acknowledged reluctantly, and wished her heart beat would slow down to a more normal rate. She moved away from Reeve uneasily, feeling his magnetism penetrate even the wall of dislike she tried to erect between them, conscious of his nearness, of her own flimsy defences, and angry at her own reaction.

'We'll give Gyp a lift back as a concession to his old bones.' Reeve moved as well, closing the gap between them until he stood beside her. 'Mrs Pugh told me where you were heading for, and I left a message for Willy at the airport to keep a lookout for us, and pick us up when he's ready.'

'You mean he'll land here? On the hill?' Surprise made Marion forget her antagonism for a moment.

'Why not?' His eyes flared with sudden laughter. 'Helicopters can go almost anywhere, and there's a small plateau just beyond the rock outcrop that's plenty big enough for Willy to put the machine on. In fact, just about here would do, it's fairly flat. Look, he's seen us already, he's cruising this way.' He raised his hand as the machine came towards them, dropping lower to land. Reeve hooked his other hand under Marion's elbow and urged her forward with him. 'I wonder what your uncle's made of the drovers' road from the air?' he murmured interestedly.

'The same as he made of it from the ground, I expect,' Marion retorted sharply. 'He'll find his map was correct, after all.' She snapped her fingers to Gyp, who rose reluctantly to his feet and ambled after them, patently preferring to doze in the sunshine for a little while longer, but her new-found concern made her prefer to keep him at her side.

'You go on, if you're in a hurry,' she tried to twist her arm free from Reeve's grip. 'I'm not riding back in the helicopter.' Her movement loosened her handkerchief from about her wrist, and it fluttered to the ground, but she left it where it was. Reeve tightened his grip on her, and she turned towards him angrily.

'Don't be silly.' He rounded on her coldly, and continued to hold her with humiliating ease. 'It's hot, and the dog's tired. And you must be too, you've had one trip up on the hill already today.'

'Take Gyp if you want to. I'm going to walk back.'

'You're going to do nothing of the kind,' he stated flatly. 'It's not safe for you to walk the hill on your own, without the dog.'

'Now who's being silly?' she scoffed. 'I've done it often enough before, and who am I likely to meet up here, in any case?' She waved a derisive hand at the surrounding landscape, empty of life except for themselves, the hovering machine, and browsing sheep.

'There's that rough-looking gypsy type. He was still slouching about when I started up the hill,' Reeve growled.

'That's only Ben Wade. I've known him since he was little,' she retorted scornfully.

'I saw you talking to him by the beck.' He sounded disapproving, as well as totally unimpressed.

'I'm as safe with him as I am with you,' she flared angrily. It was no concern of Reeve's who she talked to, she had a right to speak with whom she chose she told herself defiantly. And then she stopped, and her words died in her throat, caught on a swiftly indrawn breath as she met his steely stare.

It pinned and held her, spearlike in its intensity, halting her in her tracks as effectively as it checked her words. He reached out with his other hand and pulled her roughly towards him, the anger on his face equalling her own. She tried to pull away, but she was powerless to resist his superior strength. The breath that stopped her words seemed to desert her altogether, and her lips parted in wordless protest. She raised her eyes to his, striving to read the strange expression that rode his features like a cloud. Anger, and something else that she could not define, but she shrank from what she saw there, as much as from the words that vibrated harshly from his tight lips.

The helicopter was almost upon them, close enough to merge its shadow with their own, but despite the noise it made it failed to obliterate what he said. His words sounded in her ears with the clarity of a bell as he snapped, in clipped tones,

'What makes you think you're safe with me?'

CHAPTER EIGHT

'ALL aboard for the airport!'

Reeve released her as the pilot's cheerful voice called from the aircraft. He put her away from him, although his hand still hovered under her elbow, as if to make sure she accompanied him to the opened door of the helicopter. Willy's face beamed at them from the opening.

'Come and join us,' he invited, and held out his hand to help her.

'I'm not....' she began, in as firm a voice as she could muster—and got no further.

'You're coming back with me,' Reeve gritted in her ear from just behind. She tried to turn round, but he was too close, and she was pinned in between him and the machine, and she had no freedom to move away. He grasped her round the waist with a grip of steel, ignored her furious, 'I told you I was going to walk back!' and hoisted her bodily into the helicopter beside the pilot.

The moment her feet touched the cabin floor she spun round to jump back to the ground again, speechless with anger at his high-handed action, but with a quick snap of his fingers to Gyp he foiled her intention and sent the collie into the aircraft after her. There was no room for them both in the narrow door opening, as he must have known full well, she thought furiously, and perforce she had to wait for Gyp to scramble to safety before disembarking herself. The instant Gyp was clear of the door she moved towards it. She only took one step, and Reeve confronted her. He followed the dog into the machine without a pause, and his bulk effectively blocked her exit, forcing her to step back. He closed the door behind him with a final-sounding click, placed both hands on her arms, and propelled her firmly towards the seat.

'You sit behind Willy, I'll come beside you. Here, Gyp, under the seat boy.' He placed the dog out of the way of being stepped on and took his own seat, pulling Marion down beside him with a firm pressure. For a brief second she resisted, pride demanding she demonstrate her right to do as she pleased, and anger making her long to strike out, to free Reeve's grip from her arms.

'You can see everything from the cabin, my dear. It's quite remarkable.'

She subsided, suddenly, the choice taken from her. Short of creating a scene, Reeve left her with no option, she realised furiously. If Willy and her uncle had not been there. . . .

'Gyp doesn't seem to mind the idea of flying,' Willy spoke from in front of her. 'I thought he might have been afraid.'

'Why should he be?' Miles Dorman raised his head in innocent enquiry from his maps. 'He knows he's safe with us,' he said simply, and returned to his study.

'Marion may not have Gyp's sublime confidence,' Willy laughed. 'What about it, Marion? Are you scared?' he grinned back at her.

'Well, are you?' Reeve repeated the question softly, into the sudden silence that hovered on the heels of the pilot's question. 'Are you afraid?' he asked.

'Of course I'm not afraid of flying,' she denied stoutly. 'I've flown often enough before.' But she knew she begged the question. Willy had meant flying. Reeve had not, and his derisive glance told her so. She tried not to meet it. She tried to look away, but his silent gaze drew her with an irresistible force, and her heart thumped painfully as she met the mockery on his face, accusing her of being afraid —of him? Taunting her, because he knew.... But she dared not admit to feeling afraid, particularly with Willy and her uncle there. Particularly to herself.... Miles Dorman knew she was not afraid to fly, and if she said she was, and used that as an excuse, he would want an explanation.

'What makes you think you're safe with me?'

She could not give her uncle that as an explanation. He was quite capable, in spite of his gentle nature, of turning Reeve out of the Fleece. And with a sinking heart Marion knew she did not want him to go. Could not bear the thought of him leaving.

'I love him....'

The knowledge hit her with devastating force. How could you possibly love, and hate, and fear, all at the same time? she wondered despairingly. She tried to drag her eyes away from his, but the lurking laughter in the steel grey pools held her, drowning her.... Panic grew inside her, and she gave a convulsive tremor.

'Time we went,' Willy announced laconically from in front. He did something to the controls, the rotors spun into whirring life, and Gyp stirred restlessly from underneath the seat.

'It's all right, boy. Lie still.' Reeve bent to put a reassuring hand on the dog's head. His move took his eyes away from Marion's face, and she leaned back weakly in her seat, released as if from bondage, and trembling in every limb.

'You get a wonderful view of the drovers' road from the air, Marion.' Her uncle twisted round in his seat, completely unaware of the turmoil that possessed his niece. 'Quite different from when you're on the ground,' he enthused. 'The bits of the road we couldn't trace seem quite clear from up here.'

'Let's take Marion across and show her,' Reeve suggested, and obediently Willy turned the machine in the direction of the rock outcrop.

'You two have already seen it,' said Willy. 'Let Marion have the best view this time.' He manoeuvred the helicopter so that the rock outcrop was on Marion's side of the machine. The transparent bubble of the cabin gave her a perfect view, but suddenly she did not want to look. She knew she had to, for her uncle's sake. But Reeve was close beside her, she could feel him pressing against her, their shoulders touching in the narrow confines of the cabin. She sensed his silent insistence that she should look down, to see the route of the drovers' road, which something told her with uncompromising clarity, went to the right, and not to the left, of the rocks.

'Aren't you going to look? Or are you afraid of that, too?' He spoke so quietly that only she could hear him. She stiffened resentfully, feeling his breath fan her cheek, feeling him challenge her to look, and see, and admit that the road ran to the right of the rocks, as he said.

She looked down, and the line of the ancient road ran to the right of the rocks, as he said. It was startlingly obvious. Contours that had seemed perfectly flat from the ground stood out now in bold relief against the hillside, and the line of the ancient road ran unbroken as far as she could see on either side. Against her will her eyes traced its length to each horizon. The line to the left of the rocks was equally obviously—simply exposed rock. She sensed him stiffen, waiting for her to speak, and she compressed her lips stubbornly.

'It does go to the right of the rocks—look, Marion.' Her uncle pointed downwards, eager to show her this new wonder. 'I remember I was doubtful, at the time.'

'Are you still doubtful?' Reeve asked Marion softly in her ear.

Doubtful of what? she wondered wildly. Of the route taken by the drovers' road? Or of whether she loved him? There was no possible doubt in her mind about that. She wished fervently there could be. If she did not love Reeve, she would not feel so miserable now. But surely he could not know that? Even Reeve could not—must not—read her innermost thoughts. Then why did he lean against her so closely? She tried to move away, suffocated by the behaviour of her heart, which hammered in her breast like a wild thing beating against the bars of a cage.

'So, the road goes to the right of the rock. Now are you satisfied?' she forced the words out through clenched teeth.

'Not entirely, but it'll do for now.' Reeve leaned back in his seat, completely at ease, an enigmatic smile playing at the corners of his mouth.

Marion shot him a suspicious glance. What did he mean, it would do for now? Whatever it meant, he evidently did not intend to enlarge, and she wriggled into a more comfortable position in her own seat, trying to free herself from the consciousness of his shoulder against her own.

'Are you ready to go back now?' Willy enquired patiently from the front, and Reeve answered him calmly,

'Quite ready, if Miles is?'

So it was Miles now, not Mr Dorman. Reeve seemed to have penetrated her uncle's normal barrier of reserve more quickly than she suspected, Marion thought uneasily.

'They're haymaking in Merevale.' Miles Dorman left his maps for a moment to scan the ground over which they were passing.

'I don't see anyone doing the same in Fallbeck.' From their height it was possible to view both valleys, and with typical boyish enthusiasm Willy turned the journey into a hay-spotting competition.

'There's very little hay gathered in our valley,' Miles Dorman answered him, 'and it's always a lot later ripening than it is in Merevale. Fallbeck Scar casts a long shadow.' So did Reeve, thought Marion, and one that was infinitely more menacing than the shadow of the Scar. 'It creates a sort of micro-climate of its own,' her uncle went on meticulously, 'because for the greater part of the day it keeps the sun off the lower fields. It has the opposite effect on Merevale, of course, the rise of the hill shelters the other valley from the worst of the weather, and facing south it gets the best of both worlds, plenty of sunshine and the watershed makes sure it has adequate rain. You can see how much more fertile it is,' he pointed out, and Marion could have screamed at him.

'He's playing right into Reeve's hands,' she thought desperately. 'Have you altered the marking on your map?' she asked him aloud. She had to divert his attention somehow, or he would soon be agreeing with Reeve that Fallbeck valley would serve a more useful purpose as a reservoir, rather than as farmland.

'Yes, I've traced the proper course of the road.' Marion compressed her lips, her relief at the success of her ploy mitigated by the galling knowledge that Reeve had been right, and she had been wrong. She let her uncle's reply go by without comment. There was nothing she could say. She could feel Reeve watching her, waiting for her to speak.

'I won't give him the satisfaction,' she thought mutinously, and bent over the map her uncle held out, feigning an interest that for once she did not feel.

'I'll shade it for you as soon as we get home,' she promised. The small service would suit her purpose very well, and take her away from Reeve's presence the moment they reached the Fleece.

'That'll be a great help.' Her uncle accepted her offer with alacrity, as she knew he would, and she instantly felt guilty at using him as a shield between herself and Reeve.

'You'd better have the map now, in case I forget to give it to you when we get home.'

Marion smiled. At least her uncle knew his own shortcomings. When he had his mind on the book he was writing, he became as absentminded as a professor. Her smile vanished as, out of the corner of her eye, she saw Reeve stir in his seat and lean forward, as if he was going to take the map himself. She sat up straight and reached out and almost snatched the parchment from Miles Dorman's hand. Swiftly she rolled it into a pencil-thin tube, and slipped it up her sleeve as far as her elbow. The ribbed wrist of her sweater would effectively prevent it from falling out. It was a ruse she had used more than once with her own sketches, when prevailing hazards—and she had faced many on her various journeys over wild terrain— might take her immediate attention and make her momentarily forget her work in the face of more immediate urgencies, until it was too late to retrieve it, and her efforts had gone to waste.

She felt Reeve stiffen beside her, and knew that her move had angered him. It emanated from him in a cold aura, and she shivered under the silent, implacable force of it.

'I've got a right to the map. Uncle Miles held it out for me, not for him,' she told herself, but just the same she wished she could ride in the back seat of the car when they touched down at the airport and changed their mode of transport. But once again Reeve put her determinedly into the front passenger seat, and effectively removed any objection she might make by saying considerately to her uncle,

'You'll have more room for your papers on the back seat,' he smiled at the older man in a kindly manner, 'and there's a pull-out table if you want to work on your maps between here and the time we get to the Fleece.' He pulled down the neatly concealed folding table, deliberately pandering to her uncle's patent reluctance to waste a minute before making notes on his new-found knowledge, Marion thought furiously. He handed her into the front seat, and his hard glance dared her to defy him.

'He'll probably leave me to walk back if I do,' she shrugged resignedly, and tucked herself into the luxurious embrace of the big seat, trying to force herself to feel glad that at least Gyp was enjoying his ride. The dog curled up contentedly in the well in the back of the car with her uncle, and made it plain he approved of the novel experience by his lazily waving tail, but it did not prevent him from jumping out of the car the moment the door opened when they reached the forecourt of the Fleece, and following his nose kitchenwards with a singlemindedness of purpose that drew a laugh from Willy as he prepared to park the car in the stables at the back of the hotel.

'Well!' he exclaimed disgustedly to the back of the retreating animal, 'he might at least have stopped to say thank you!'

'I'll leave Marion to make amends for him,' smiled her uncle, and courteously thanking Reeve himself, he disappeared in the direction of his study, leaving Marion reluctantly facing Reeve across the narrow hall.

'Thank you.' She made amends as briefly as possible.

'Is that all?' he asked her, and his tone was as steely as his eyes.

'What else is there to say?'

'You could say you're sorry,' he suggested coldly.

'Whatever for?' She gazed at him in angry astonishment. If he thought she was going to apologise for being wrong about the route of the drovers' road, he was very much mistaken. 'I've got nothing to feel sorry for,' she told him adamantly.

'I'll soon remedy that,' he growled.

All the pent-up anger that he had held until now under rigid control released itself in his kiss. His lips descended on hers with a bruising force. She struggled and tried to break away, but his arms encircled her like a vice, and her strength was as nothing against their power. She arched her back, trying to force herself away from him, but the pressure of his lips did not slacken, until the burning heat of his kiss melted her resistance, and in spite of her fury she felt herself begin to yield. Her body became pliant in his arms, responding against her will, the treacherous fire running once again through her veins until it blotted out everything but the feel of his arms around her, his lips pressing against her own....

'Feel sorry for that!' he ground out, and pushed her away from him.

For a second he stared down at her, saw her hands rise to her face, her eyes registering the shock of what he had done, and then he turned abruptly on his heel and left her. Through a dark haze she heard the outer door slam, with a force that brought a back-draught of air against her hot cheeks. Her fingers clung to them, as if covering the sting of a blow, and they burned as if with a fever, although her body felt icy cold.

She shivered, and the violent tremor brought returned consciousness of her surroundings, and an awareness that she could not remain in the hall for the rest of the evening. She turned towards the stairs, and began to mount them on legs that felt as if they did not belong to her. She did not know where Reeve had gone to, but soon he would have to come upstairs as well, to change for dinner. The thought spurred her failing strength, and she reached the landing and the sanctuary of her own room with a sob of relief. Her strength deserted her then. Her bed held out soft arms to cushion her fall, and her pillow received the scalding outflow that she could no longer control.

Eventually her sobs lessened and died away, but she lay where she had fallen, exhausted by a storm of intensity such as she had never experienced before. Gradually she became aware of the discomfort of her wet pillow beneath her cheek, and she turned over restlessly and lay supine, bereft of the strength to get up, until the rich smell of cooking that had homed Gyp kitchenwards—how long ago was it, now? a lifetime?—drifted through her open window, a pungent reminder that somehow she must soon find the energy to rise and go downstairs, and face Mrs Pugh's sharp eyes, and try to make believe that nothing was amiss, when her whole world had crumbled in ruins about her feet.

'I've taken your uncle's meal into his study,' Mrs Pugh clicked her tongue disapprovingly. 'I can't part him from his maps, so I might as well take him his food in there and be done.'

'In that case, let's stay here and eat ours,' Marion suggested quickly. 'it'll save laying our own dining room table just for the two of us,' she begged. Suddenly she wanted to remain in the kitchen. It was warm and comforting, and represented security.

'It'll help if we do,' Mrs Pugh conceded. 'Mr Harland and Willy were a bit later coming in to their meal tonight, I can serve them and us at the same time if we stay in here.'

Luck seemed to be with her, Marion decided dully, as faced with her own good dinner and a total reluctance to eat it, she was able to deposit most of the contents of her plate on the glowing coals of the fire as soon as Mrs Pugh disappeared to take the first course in to their guests.

'There, I said a day out would do you good,' the housekeeper exclaimed on her return, seeing Marion apparently finishing off the last mouthful with relish. 'It's given you an appetite—and about time, too!' She bustled towards the oven where her own dinner was keeping hot, and Marion heaved a small sigh of relief. The light make-up she applied before coming down, and which she rarely wore, was evidently a sufficient disguise for the signs of distress that soap and cold water had not been able to fully erase.

She was drying the crockery with a listless disinterest after the meal was over when she became aware of a louder than usual noise from the public part of the house. She hung a jug back on its hook on the dresser and paused to listen.

'Someone seems to be having an argument in the bar.' Her forehead creased into a frown.

'Jim can handle anything that's likely to crop up in the bar,' Mrs Pugh retorted firmly, and Marion picked up a plate and resumed her work. The housekeeper was right, of course. Trouble in the bar of the Fleece was almost non-existent, and even under normal circumstances she knew that neither her uncle nor Mrs Pugh liked her to go in there. She pandered to their rather old-fashioned point of view readily enough. She had no desire to frequent the public rooms of the house, and her work kept her spare time amply occupied, but tonight ... The crease across her forehead deepened. More than one voice seemed to be raised, indeed there was a swelling volume of sound that augured trouble.

'D'you think I ought to call Uncle Miles?' she began, when a sharp rap sounded on the kitchen door, and the face of Jim, the barman, peered round it, bearing a frown as deep as Marion's own.

'Can you come in a minute, Miss Marion?' He sounded as worried as he looked. 'I've got a bar full of folk tonight.' That was unusual enough in itself these days, thought Marion with a prick of apprehension. 'And they're all looking for trouble,' he did nothing to allay her fears. 'They're all asking for you,' he said.

'For me?' She stared at him, uncomprehending. 'What do they want me for?'

'I dunno, miss. They keep on about something to do with the beck. I can't make head nor tail of what they're talking about,' the barman admitted helplessly.

'I'll come.' Quickly Marion slipped the bow on the back of her apron, and draped it across the back of a chair.

'Do you think you ought to, Marion?' Mrs Pugh moved across the kitchen towards her uneasily. 'Let me go and fetch your uncle,' she urged.

'Time enough to bring Uncle Miles into it when I've found out what they want me for,' Marion said with a briskness she was far from feeling. 'You stay here,' she told the housekeeper, 'I'll come back and let you know what it's all about in a minute or two. In the meantime,' she instructed firmly, 'leave Uncle Miles in peace until we know whether it's worth disturbing him or not,' she said hopefully.

'They're all steamed up about whatever it is,' Jim said gloomily as he opened the door that led into the public bar.

'I can see that.' The place was indeed full to capacity. Marion's surprised eyes picked out John Cornish, the schoolteacher; Zilla Wade, who despite her forthright habit of speech usually left her menfolk to enjoy the hospitality of the Fleece alone; the postmistress. Surely not the post-mistress? Marion looked again, but her eyes had not deceived her. Even the local vicar was there. The sight of the vicar calmed her apprehension somewhat.

'Tha' took tha' time acomin'!'

'I came as soon as I was asked.' She did not like Aaron Wade any more than she liked his wife and son, and her withering glance told him so. 'What is it you want?'

He seemed to be the self-appointed spokesman, and with a courage she did not know she possessed, she tackled the unprepossessing farmer head on. The day had already produced enough difficulties on its own, she felt, without adding a controversy with the Wades.

'We wants to know about this dam thing.'

'What thing?' She could not see anything in his hand. 'And don't use bad language in here,' she snapped, 'you know my uncle won't put up with it.'

'Dad ain't swearing.' Ben Wade shouldered his way through the crowd in the bar until he stood beside his father, and Marion realised how very much alike the two were. The comparison did not flatter either of them, she thought critically. 'He's talking about those two blokes you've got staying here. The ones who're going to build a dam across the beck, and turn the valley into a reservoir.'

How did he know? She stared at him in consternation. It was obvious that he did, and the rest of the people in the bar as well. That must be why they were there in such numbers. Realisation gripped her like a cold hand. They had come to the Fleece as the nearest public place to hold an indignation meeting, about something that was supposed to be still a secret.

'Is it true, Miss Marion?' The quiet question came from the husband of their own daily help. Marion had not noticed him before, but he too edged forward, and she found herself facing a sea of faces, some anxious, some angry, the Wades belligerent as usual, but all awaiting her answer.

'What about my farm?' Aaron Wade shouted at her angrily. 'What'll happen to that, if they has their way and floods the valley?'

'What'll happen to our homes?'

'What's going to happen to the school? My job?' That was from John Cornish, whose eyes, thought Marion with quick compassion, looked haunted with worry.

'Is that why they won't renew my Post Office licence?' The postmistress seemed to have shed her normally timid nature, and spoke up boldly with the rest.

Marion stood helpless before the avalanche of questions.

'Is it true? What's going to happen?' And the question she herself had asked, repeated from the crowd over and over again, 'Why us?'

'I don't know.' She pressed frantic fingers to her suddenly throbbing temples.

'Tha' must know. The men are staying here, aren't they?' It was Aaron Wade again, aggressive as ever, and shouting louder than the others. 'Tha' must have known afore us,' he accused her bitterly, 'but I suppose it paid to keep tha' mouth shut, seeing as they was staying at the Fleece,' he sneered.

'I only learned about it this morning.' With commendable outward calm she held up her hand for silence. Inside, she felt anything but calm. Her mind was a seething mass of questions, that ran along the same lines as their own, but with another one added for good measure. How had they found out?

'Do you expect us to believe that?' Aaron Wade growled.

'Shut up, Aaron!'

Their daily help's husband came to her aid. He was a quiet man by nature, Marion knew him slightly, but nevertheless he was a brawny quarryman, and a force to be reckoned with if put to the test. To Marion's relief Aaron Wade did not try. He subsided into sullen silence, and with a grateful glance at her helper she went on clearly.

'As I said, I only learned of it myself this morning, and if you keep quiet and listen,' she stilled a spate of mutters from the farmer, 'I'll tell you all I know.'

She accepted John Cornish's offer of a high bar stool with a grateful smile. Its height gave her a slight confidence, which helped her composure, and the seat attended to the sudden problem of trembling knees that affected her at the worst possible moment.

'I must be strong,' she whispered to herself. 'I mustn't weaken now.' She raised her head and let her glance rove across the faces in front of her, familiar each one of them, and the stillness in the bar room could be felt.

'To start with, when Mr Harland and his pilot booked in at the Fleece, we did not know the reason why they were in the district. We could not have refused them accommodation even if we had known,' she emphasised, and raised her voice above a disbelieving snort from the farmer. 'When we learned that they were here to survey the valley for the purpose of building a reservoir, Mr Harland assured us that nothing definite had yet been decided. A survey has been carried out, and a recommendation made to the local authority, but that's all.' She sounded almost as if she was defending Reeve, she thought with amazement.

'And now tha' does know, what's tha' going to do about it?' Aaron Wade wanted to know.

'I can't do anything about it on my own,' Marion retorted sharply. 'If the recommendation is turned down, and they take their reservoir somewhere else, there'll be no need to do anything.' Her voice reflected her total lack of conviction, and with a sinking heart she saw her audience sensed it. 'If the recommendation is accepted, and they decide to use Fallbeck valley for their reservoir,' the expressions tensed, watching, waiting. From behind her she heard the click of a door opening and then shutting again. Perhaps her uncle had joined them, he always came to be with the barman for a while before closing time, and tonight he must have chosen to come in earlier than usual. Perhaps Mrs Pugh had sent for him, after all.

'We'll all have to make a stand together, and fight for

the valley,' she concluded sturdily.

The continuing silence when she finished speaking puzzled her. She had expected an immediate buzz of conversation to break out. Argument, possibly suggestions. But not this awful silence. It seemed to go on and on. It was unnerving. She scanned the faces confronting her, and realised that they were no longer looking at her. The sea of eyes were fixed on something—someone—behind her. She swivelled round on her stool.

'Admirably put,' Reeve congratulated her icily. 'You didn't lose much time, did you?' His eyes bored into hers, ignoring the other people pressing about them, and the contempt in his face lashed her like a whip.

'So this is how you keep your promise not to say anything until something definite is known?' he flung at her harshly.

CHAPTER NINE

'I DIDN'T say anything to anybody,' Marion protested indignantly. 'Jim called me to come....'

'Do you expect me to believe that?' He repeated Aaron Wade's question almost word for word. 'I saw you talking to Ben Wade this afternoon when I followed you up the hill. I don't doubt he made an efficient town crier,' he said sarcastically.

'I said nothing to Ben about the dam,' she denied hotly. 'He'll tell you what we were talking about when we saw one another by the beck.' She turned to the youth who stood near them, listening to the exchange with a sly grin on his face. 'You know I said nothing about the possibility of a reservoir being built here,' she appealed to him.

'Who's to say what we talked about by the beck?' Ben's black eyes roved insolently over her flushed face. 'There was only you and me to hear, and the dogs,' he gave a wink and his grin broadened, and Marion stared at him furiously. She should have known better than to appeal to him, his nature was as spiteful as his mother's. 'We all know about it now anyway,' he added maliciously, 'so that's that.'

'So now you know.' Reeve leaned against the bar and surveyed the room. In his manner was nothing of aggression, nor challenge—nor guilt, thought Marion angrily, at what he was doing to their small community. Just a calm confidence, and an air of authority that stilled the buzz of talk and brought every eye in the room on to him.

'Nothing can be done until the local authority have had time to study the report, and decide one way or the other,' he went on clearly.

'Was the recommendation yours?' John Cornish asked quietly.

'Yes.' He did not attempt to dodge the responsibility, thought Marion with reluctant admiration.

'And it was ... ?'

'That Fallbeck valley should be used for the reservoir,' he answered.

A hiss of expelled breath rippled across the room, like the portent of a storm to come.

'He don't try to duck out of the way of trouble, does he?' Jim the barman breathed in awe.

'It's as well he doesn't,' Marion retorted grimly, 'he's likely to get enough come his way over this.'

'Here's the first broadside coming up now.'

The last of Jim's prophecy was drowned by Aaron Wade's shout.

'No one's taking my farm away from me without a fight!' he blustered.

'What will become of the school, Mr Harland?'

'Aye, what about the kids?' The farmer took up John Cornish's question eagerly.

'And the church,' the vicar raised his voice amongst the others.

'One at a time.' Reeve followed suit, and gradually the

uproar subsided. He spoke calmly into the ensuing silence. 'If it's decided to proceed with the reservoir,' he stressed the 'if', 'your farm will be the subject of individual negotiation, as will each of the separate homes and holdings,' he told the farmer straightly.

'Individual negotiation my foot!' came a voice from the back of the crowd—one of the local smallholders, Marion saw. 'Miss Dorman said we all had to make a stand together.'

'That wouldn't be possible as regards compensation.' Reeve seemed completely unruffled by the heckling, and Marion wondered what he was feeling underneath. He had probably met the same kind of opposition many times. And crushed it, she thought bitterly. 'Miss Dorman must know that each holding would command a different sum of money.' He paused slightly, then added deliberately, 'She read my recommendation.'

'I only read the first bit,' Marion cried indignantly, but Aaron Wade interrupted her angrily.

'You didn't tell us you've read what he's writ,' he snarled at her vengefully, and she shrank from the vindictive look he shot at her.

'As to the school,' Reeve quelled the farmer with a glance, and addressed John Cornish, 'I understand that it's already in danger of being closed for lack of pupils. There are two sets of twins due to be transferred to school in Dale End this autumn—isn't that what you told me, Marion?' He turned to her courteously for confirmation— on purpose, Marion felt sure, to impress the people in the room with the accuracy of his source of information.

She felt her colour begin to rise, then it flamed suddenly as Aaron Wade turned on her furiously.

'You're not content with keeping him and his pilot under your roof,' he gestured towards Reeve angrily, 'but you have to supply him with all the information he wants as well. I wonder what other favours you've shown him,' he hinted spitefully.

'Now, Aaron, there's no call for that. . . .'

'Another remark like that,' Reeve straightened away from his leaning post on the bar, and towered over the farmer, and his voice cut like a rapier, 'another remark like that, and you'll find yourself outside the door,' he promised evenly.

'When you asked me all those questions, I'd no idea why you wanted the information.' Marion dissociated herself angrily from such Quisling activity. Aaron Wade was an offensive boor, but she did not need Reeve to defend her, she thought passionately. He was an excellent strategist, though, she acknowledged caustically. By one well-timed remark he had managed to implant doubt in the minds of the very people who would have listened to her : who would have been welded together by her in a common interest. And now the doubt was there it would be impossible to eradicate it, she realised that, too. With one master stroke, he had succeeded in alienating her from the rest of the crowd.

His action reminded her irresistibly of the words of a tall, sun-bronzed ranger whom she had met in the South African bush on one of her copy-searching missions. Noticing her interest, he gave her the benefit of his knowledge of the habits of various predators, hunting game often larger than themselves.

'There isn't much they can do against a united herd,' he explained, 'the hunters would probably only get themselves trampled for their pains. But they're wily, they try to scatter the herd if they can, and then they're able to pick them off one by one at their leisure.'

That was exactly what Reeve was doing now. Splitting the crowd, and taking on one at a time. And if he negotiated with each one separately, in their own houses, and behind closed doors where the others could not hear, she knew what would happen, she thought despairingly. The offer of a large sum of money in compensation—perhaps the fear that it might be reduced if they remained until they were forced out—and self-interest would do the rest. It would only need one or two to lose their nerve and pack up and leave, for the defences of the others to crumble at a touch. And Reeve would provide the touch.

'I hate you for this!' she whispered passionately. She loved him, but she hated him too, with all the fiery force of her nature that longed to strike aside the hand which threatened to tear apart the very fabric of their valley. He heard her words. She could tell by the way he stiffened, and half turned towards her, and then the vicar repeated his question.

'What about the church?'

'I haven't seen it up close yet,' Reeve answered him frankly, 'but I'm told on good authority,' this time he did turn, and slanted a glance directly at Marion, continuing his tactics of scattering the herd, she thought caustically, 'I'm told on good authority that the building itself is architecturally uninteresting.' He repeated her own words with sarcastic emphasis.

She felt, rather than saw, the vicar's shocked look, straight across the room at her. Accusing. She paled with anger.

'What are you trying to do?' she whispered to Reeve furiously. 'Make them hate me?' Sensitive to atmospheres, she could feel an almost tangible change towards her in the room. The easy acceptance of her as one of themselves, which she was accorded when she first joined the crowd in the bar, had disappeared, and in its place was a wary withdrawal, a barrier of mistrust put there, she realised angrily, by Reeve's insidious barbs, each one of which had found its intended target.

'You can't touch a church,' Aaron Wade shouted triumphantly. 'Whether it's archi—archi—whatever you said or not, you can't touch a church. No one'd stand for it,' he concluded confidently.

'People fight for what they value.' Reeve's eyes bored into the farmer's, and Marion noticed Wade *père*'s look falter and drop away beneath the undisguised contempt on his face.

'Do you go to church?' Reeve enquired silkily. 'Well, do

you?' when no response was forthcoming.

'I—er—well. . . .' The uneasy mutter trailed into confused silence.

'What, Dad go to church?' Ben had no inhibitions about speaking the truth this time, if only to aggravate his father. 'He ain't been near the place since the day I was christened,' he jeered derisively.

'And because of the scattered community, the same probably applies to half the valley,' Reeve thrust his point home. 'There just aren't that many people left in Fallbeck valley any more, there's only a quarter of the population here now that it supported fifty years ago. And only a third of those actually live in the village, within reasonable reach of the church. The rest are scattered at a distance far enough away to make them think twice before coming into the village for a service, particularly in the winter, and if they've got milking to attend to.' He had a valid point there, Marion admitted reluctantly. All the farms were family concerns, invariably shorthanded, and cows had no respect for the timing of church services.

'There's weddings and christenings and such.' Aaron Wade was determined not to give in.

'There hasn't been a wedding in the church for the last five years.' Reeve had the attention of the room on him now, Marion could feel the stiffening of interest at the cut and thrust of the exchange. 'And what's worse,' he paused, and his glance flicked over the raised faces, 'at least to me it seems worse,' he commented grimly, 'there hasn't been a christening in the church for eleven years.'

'There's kids at the school younger'n eleven,' the farmer began.

'You're out of touch,' Reeve assured him coldly. 'The last babies christened in Fallbeck were the younger of the two sets of twins. The other children came to the valley when they were older, with their parents. They belong to two families,' he let the facts drop one by one like a stone into a deepening pool of silence. 'Their fathers are brothers who both came back to live in the valley so

that they could help on their own father's smallholding
when he got too old to work it himself. They're both
quarrymen by trade, with no real interest in the farm
beyond a filial loyalty, and they work it in their spare
time between them. How long do you think they're likely
to remain in the valley when they're no longer obliged to,
by family ties?' Reeve asked, leaning forward to empha-
sise his point. 'They'll do the same as the other young
couples who've married in Fallbeck,' he prophesied, 'they'll
leave the valley to find work and a life for themselves outside. Somewhere where there's a bus service, so that the
schools and churches and shops can be reached easily,
without half a day's journey to get there, and no matter
what the weather. And that will take the last of the pupils
from the school, he thrust his point home.

Marion could see from the expression of his audience
that in this one thing at least, most of them agreed with
him.

'You've been thorough, haven't you?' Her bitter comment sliced across the following silence, and evoked a
response from Aaron Wade.

'We'll put a stop to tha' plans,' he growled at Reeve
threateningly. 'We'll put tha' helicopter out of action, so
you'll regret ever bringing it here....'

'Don't be silly!' Marion spun round on the farmer,
frightened by what he might say next. Frightened that his
suggestion might take hold. 'You can't go around damaging
people's property—you'll get yourself arrested.' It might
not stop at property, she thought worriedly. Aaron Wade
had a notoriously unstable temper, and what started as
malicious damage to property could escalate. Reeve could
take care of himself, she felt sure, but.... Her mind refused
to contemplate a worse possibility.

'What's he going to do to our property?' the farmer
shouted back, glowering at Reeve. 'I suppose you think
drowning a village with water is legal and right?' His
face was rapidly becoming purple. 'Of course, tha'll stick
up for him.'

'I wasn't. . . .'

'That's enough, Aaron!'

'Take him home, Zilla, afore he gets himself into trouble,' their daily's husband suggested sensibly.

Marion stole a look at Reeve. He stood beside the bar, tight-lipped, his body taut like a bow string, facing the angry flood of question and counter-question, threat and argument. Without thinking, she backed against the bar next to him and gazed at the familiar faces in front of her, that suddenly seemed strange, and hostile. Any minute now there might be a fight . . . Reeve's bulk beside her felt distinctly reassuring.

'Time, gentlemen, please!'

The barman defused the situation with beautiful simplicity.

It was almost farcical the way the noise ceased, and sheer habit took over. There was a startled pause, a moment of empty silence, then glasses clinked on table tops, and a gradual stirring began towards the door. One or two 'goodnights' were exchanged, and then unbelievably the bar-room emptied, and through a fog Marion heard Jim lock the outer door.

'Are you feeling all right, Miss Marion?' Jim's kindly voice penetrated the daze that seemed to possess her mind, and she nodded dumbly. She felt anything but all right. Now the tension had gone, she shook all over. Her ashen face gave the lie to her bravado, and with a keen glance at her, Reeve took her by the arm.

'Come on,' he pulled her upright and held her against him with a firm grip. 'Back to Mrs Pugh,' he commanded.

Somehow her legs obeyed him, even though her mind resented his command.

'Where's Uncle Miles?' A spark of defiance made her pause. She could not see her uncle anywhere in the room.

'I told him not to bother to come down, I'd see to whatever was going on here.'

'You told him . . .?' She choked on his usurped authority. 'You'd no right!' she began indignantly.

'Would you rather I'd let him face that crowd? Aaron Wade?' he asked silkily.

'No—no, of course not.' She would rather anything happen than that. Anything, except that Reeve should take over.

'And since I'm the only available target they've got as regards the reservoir, I consider I've got every right.'

She felt too shaken for the moment to argue with him. Somehow she responded to Jim's 'Goodnight, miss,' and the next she knew Reeve's hands pressed her down into the big armchair by the drawing room fire, and Mrs Pugh abandoned her knitting to pour out coffee for them both.

'I can see it wasn't easy in there,' she remarked with a searching glance at Marion's face.

'It was mostly Aaron Wade,' she began wearily. 'He went on and on about his farm, and the church....' She took a hurried gulp of coffee to cover the humiliating quaver in her voice.

'What, Aaron Wade stand up for the church?' Mrs Pugh snorted scornfully. 'He's a funny one to do that, and no mistake. He's kept up a running fight with three vicars in a row for the last twenty odd years, and all because he let one of his cows eat yew from a tree in the churchyard, and it died. It was his own carelessness that did it, but he blamed the vicar at the time, and he's taken it out on the other two who've had the living because of it. He wears a grudge like a coat, does that man,' she declared waspishly.

That just about summed up the whole Wade family, thought Marion, and dropped her head back tiredly against the chair cushions.

'Well, I'm off to bed now things have quietened down.' Mrs Pugh stifled a yawn behind a plump hand. 'And from the look of you, you'd best be doing the same,' she advised Marion.

'I'll come up with you.' Marion started to pull herself up from her chair. She did not want to make the effort, but she did not want to be left alone with Reeve, either.

'Finish your coffee first.' Reeve nodded pleasantly to the housekeeper, and put Marion's refilled cup back into her hands. She had not asked for another cup, but she had to take it or risk a spill. He stood half in front of her chair, effectively preventing her from rising, and she watched the housekeeper close the door behind her with a feeling of inevitability.

'I suppose you feel satisfied now?' She spoke in a hard voice, into the silence that followed Mrs Pugh's departure. She leaned forward to put her coffee cup on the table near to her chair, her movement obliging Reeve to stand aside. It gave her a small satisfaction that he had to move away, and rejecting her unwanted coffee gave her another. She did not intend to drink it just because Reeve had given it to her.

'You effectively scattered the herd,' she added bitterly, almost to herself. Reeve would not understand the inference, but what did it matter? She underestimated his perception.

'Surely that's the best tactic, when you're fighting single-handed?' He took her point immediately, and pulling up the chair opposite to her he leaned back and crossed his legs comfortably. Marion noticed the knife-edge creases in his perfectly pressed slacks.

'Not so far as I'm concerned, it isn't.' She spoke quickly, reaction to the strain she had been subjected to undermining her caution. 'You deliberately made it look as if I sided with you. As if I knew about the reservoir all along, and supplied you with all sorts of information.' She swallowed convulsively, and started again with difficulty. 'They'll all look on me as some sort of traitor,' she burst out hotly.

'Not for long, they won't.' Reeve seemed completely uncaring of what he had done, and its possible consequences for her, she thought heatedly. 'It'll be a nine days' wonder, then it'll die down, and life will go on just the same.'

'How can it, if you flood the valley?'

'We were talking about your relationship with the valley

people,' he reminded her blandly.

'I probably haven't got any relationships left with them now, thanks to you.'

'Do you want them, Marion?' he asked her quietly, and in his voice was an underlying something that brought her eyes up to his in startled surprise. He uncrossed his legs and leaned forward in his chair, his arms resting on his knees, and his eyes bored into her own, questioning, demanding an answer. But she neither knew what the question was, nor what she was supposed to answer. When he looked at her like that her mind went blank. Her powers of reasoning deserted her, and her own feelings threatened to overwhelm her. She dared not give way to them now. Above all, she must not allow Reeve to suspect how she felt towards him. It would undermine her power to fight the plans he had for the valley. If only he had come to the Fleece as an ordinary guest, she thought miserably, how different things might have been then.

'Of course I want them,' she spoke forcefully, trying by words to blot out the train of her thoughts. 'They're my people.'

'They're not.' He contradicted her patiently, like someone trying to reason with an obstructive child, she thought angrily. 'You belong to Miles. Possibly,' he smiled, 'you also belong to Mrs Pugh. But not to the valley people. You can't argue otherwise,' he stilled her protest and went on confidently, 'you weren't brought up in the valley, and now your work, your whole way of life, lies outside it.'

'I came back to live here.' She dared not allow him to go on, what he said was the truth, and she must not admit it, even to herself.

'Only as a temporary measure, to be with your uncle until he found his feet again after his wife died. And he appears to be coping very well, probably the book he's writing has helped.'

Implying that her presence at the Fleece was no longer necessary. Sudden tears pricked the back of her eyes. Fatigue, and strain, and the treacherous morass of her

own emotions, took their toll, and she felt a weak desire
to cry. She blinked hard several times, and managed to
force the tears back. She must not let them fall in front of
Reeve, he would scorn her weakness, and regard it as
another victory, one of many individual victories which he
would win in order to take over the valley. If only things
were different, and she could cry out her troubles against
his shoulder, let the tears fall, and feel his arms go round
her, comforting her. Hear his deep, calm voice assure
her that all would be well, and believe it, because he said
so. . . .

'You'll soon have to make a decision one way or another,
about staying on with your uncle.' Brutally he forced her
to look at something which she had manged to push to the
back of her mind for many weeks, a growing realisation that
her time at the Fleece was nearing its end, and she must
soon make up her mind to take up the threads of her old
life again. In the face of a family emergency, the decision
to abandon it had not seemed too difficult. Now, her previous existence of constant travel and new faces, that had
seemed so interesting before, held out no attraction to her.
Life without Reeve held no attraction.

'Even if the reservoir project doesn't go ahead, would
you be content to remain here in the valley indefinitely?'
he persisted. 'Among the valley people? Do you really have
enough in common with any of them to make you want
to stay? All those who are left are either a lot older or a
lot younger than you are. Ben Wade's about the only one
who's anywhere near your own age.' His expression told
Marion quite plainly what he thought of Ben Wade as a
suitable companion for her.

'I'm quite capable of making my own decisions,' she
snapped. 'And finding my own friends, without your
help.' She jumped to her feet abruptly, and her hands
came up in an instinctive gesture, as if to ward off his
questions. Or to ward off the answers that she found she
did not want to listen to? Frighteningly, she discovered
she did not even like the valley people much any more. The

glimpse she received of their faces in the uproar of the bar-room had classed them all as strangers, with whom she had nothing in common, not even the fight for their homes.

Reeve was right—again—she admitted despairingly. She had no place in the valley. It was she who was the stranger, not the valley people. She did not belong, except to her uncle and Mrs Pugh. But they were family, and did not count.

'Why did you have to come here, upsetting everything?' she cried passionately. 'Everything was peaceful until you came.' She had not made any close friends in the valley, but she had not made any enemies either, and now, she realised with a sick feeling of dismay, she had probably made more than one of the latter after the events in the bar-room that evening. Until Reeve arrived, her work had been sufficient to keep her happy. Now that was spoiled too, because of him. She found it difficult to forgive him for spoiling her joy in her work.

'My being here doesn't alter the fact that you'd have had to make a decision about leaving your uncle and resuming your own life sooner or later.' He spoke sharply, as if her thrust had gone home.

'Whether or not I decide to stay with Uncle Miles is none of your business,' she retorted angrily. 'Because you're trying to take over the valley, it doesn't give you the right to take over our family life as well.' He could take over her own life any time he pleased, simply for the asking, she thought drearily. But he would not ask. She had made an enemy of Reeve, as well as the rest of the valley.

'I'm going to bed. I'm too tired to stand here and argue with you. Goodnight.'

She turned abruptly towards the door. He rose as she came to his chair and stood silently watching her. She paused. She did not want to. She wanted to sweep out of the door and slam it behind her, but her feet would not obey her will. They obeyed her treacherous heart instead, and brought her to a dragging halt, facing him. Why was it she had to remember so clearly what happened the last time they were in this room together? To feel his arms around her—her whole body ached for the feel of his arms. Her look was unconsciously appealing, but it did not soften Reeve's expression. He looked back at her, making no move to touch her, but standing rigidly apart, and his voice was as hard as his face as he replied curtly,

'Goodnight!'

Just that, and nothing more. She winced as if he had struck her. The pain of the blow that did not fall galvanised her feet into action. Unerringly they carried her through the door she could no longer see, up the stairs that felt as steep as the fellside by the waterfall, and into the blessed privacy of her own room, where her brimming eyes spilled over, and she tried with desperate hands to stifle the sobs that racked her shaking body until it felt as if her heart must surely break.

CHAPTER TEN

SHE awoke the next day with a headache. Sleep eluded her until the early hours of the morning, the torment of her mind denying her exhausted body rest, until the first faint streaks of daylight appeared through the curtains, and she finally dropped into an uneasy doze. As a result, she slept late.

'Heavens, is that the time?'

By now she had usually taken Gyp for a walk and had a critical look at her previous day's work on the woodcut to see if there was any final touching up to be done before she took it a stage further.

'Where's the haste?' Mrs Pugh enquired placidly when she hurried downstairs, tugging her sweater into place over her slacks with fumbling fingers.

'Gyp hasn't had his walk yet.'

'Gyp took himself off for a walk, when you didn't appear,' the housekeeper told her comfortably.

'On his own?' Marion looked up sharply. 'Where is he now? Has he come back?' Alarm bells rang in her mind, and she looked round the kitchen urgently.

'Of course he's come back,' Mrs Pugh answered mildly. 'He wasn't gone five minutes. You know he won't stir until he's had the bacon rinds when I'm cooking breakfast.' An appetising smell of smoked bacon came from the direction of the grill. 'He reckons they're his starters for the day, the same as our cup of tea is for us, don't you boy?' She scraped the rinds into a feeding bowl standing in a corner of the kitchen floor, and the sound brought a long grin and a happily waving tail through the door, and the dog made straight for the awaited titbit. Marion heaved a sigh of pure relief. Ben Wade's warning had done its work well, she thought ruefully. She found she was trembling.

'Come and have your own cup of tea, now.' Mrs Pugh gave her a searching look, and drew her own conclusions from the dark rings that made smoky hollows under Marion's eyes, in telling contrast to her white face.

'I'll take him for a proper walk when I've had my cup of tea,' she promised. She curled grateful fingers round the warmth of the cup, glad of its comfort. She felt unaccountably shivery since she got up, probably because she was tired.

'You can take him when you've had some breakfast, not until,' unexpectedly Mrs Pugh put her foot down. 'It's no good walking the hill if you've got no food inside you,' she said sensibly, and at any other time Marion would have wholeheartedly agreed with her. This morning the last thing she felt in need of was food. 'And if you're going on the hill, take your mac with you,' the housekeeper continued, 'the weather forecast says there's rain on the way later today.'

'It's bright enough now.'

'Best do as she says, miss,' a cheerful voice from the doorway agreed with the housekeeper, and the milkman reached inside and put half a dozen bottles tidily on the slab provided for the purpose. 'My gammy leg's been playing up ever since last night, and it's never let me down yet about the weather.' He limped off, whistling, taking with him his shortened limb, the result of a severe break, which proved a remarkably accurate barometer on which most of his customers had come to depend.

'Just a piece of toast will be enough.' She hurriedly prevented Mrs Pugh from preparing a generous helping of bacon and eggs for her consumption. 'They'll do for the dining room.' Reeve and Willy would eat them, she doubted if either Reeve's sleep or his appetite had been impaired because of last night's episode, she thought tartly, and wondered whether she meant when he was facing the crowded bar-room, or later, when he was in the drawing room, alone with her. With an effort she pushed the thought of him from her mind. The fact that it was an effort annoyed her irrationally, and she sighed with impatient exasperation. His image seemed to be indelibly imprinted on her thoughts, and she could not erase it.

'I must do something about it,' she muttered irritably.

'Why, is something wrong with your woodcut?' Mrs Pugh enquired, and Marion realised she must have spoken out loud. She really would have to take herself in hand, she decided, Reeve had got her talking to herself now.

'No, there's nothing wrong. Just something I mustn't forget to do,' she prevaricated.

'I thought it was coming along nicely the last time I looked at it.' Mrs Pugh took a good deal of interest in her work, and until now Marion had welcomed her friendly helpfulness.

'It's coming along fine,' she declared untruthfully. Since Reeve had been staying at the Fleece, she had scarcely touched it. 'I'll do an hour or two's work on it later today, I'll take Gyp for his walk first.' She did not feel inclined to work with her chisels while her fingers trembled so. She dared not risk spoiling what she had done so far. She surreptitiously slipped the last of her unwanted toast between the dog's willing jaws and escaped from the kitchen and Mrs Pugh's all-seeing eye.

'Don't forget your mac,' the older woman called after her.

'I won't,' Marion called back, and turned towards the door which led into the public part of the house. Her mac hung on the hallstand there, she had forgotten to take it back to her room. It would be easy enough to reach it while Reeve and Willy were in the dining room, and she could go out by the front door. She was half way into the hall when she heard Reeve's voice speak to Willy from the landing at the head of the stairs.

'I'll come up with you today for an hour or so.'

She did not wait to hear any more. She clicked her fingers urgently to the dog, and backed hurriedly out again. 'Come on, Gyp, this way!' To her relief he followed her without his usual friendly woof of response. He was still crunching the last of her toast, and it effectively kept him silent as he cavorted about her feet. She closed the door behind her, and thought quickly. If she went out through the walled garden, she could use the gate in the wall and the footpath beyond it to gain the fells. It would take her a bit out of her way, but it would mean a longer walk for Gyp, so he would not mind, and as Reeve was coming downstairs with Willy he would not see her through his bedroom window, which like her own looked out over the garden. She breathed more freely as she closed the outer door behind her, the walled garden made a perfumed sanctuary effectively covering her retreat.

'Leave Tibby alone, you bully!' she scolded as Gyp, his toast safely swallowed, made a noisy rush at the tabby cat. It fled spitting for the wall, its tail fluffed out like a bottle brush, and Marion grabbed the dog's collar and hauled him away. 'She's out of reach, so leave her in peace,' she commanded sternly. The tabby settled on the top of the garden wall, secure among the climbing roses, which Marion saw with a pang of regret were already beginning to fade with the advancing summer. There would perhaps be one more vase full of buds to pick, and that would be all until the second blooming in the autumn. Where would they all be, then? she wondered bleakly. 'Go on, run off some of your energy.' She let the dog out of the door in the wall, and followed more slowly herself. 'You ought to be ashamed, chasing cats at your age,' she gave his ears an affectionate rub as she released him. 'You're behaving like a two-year-old!' But if he was still spry enough to enjoy chasing the cat, might he not also enjoy chasing sheep? she wondered worriedly.

She skirted a patch of cotton grass, avoiding the swampy ground that its presence betrayed, and absentmindedly noted that the small white tufts lay almost horizontal against the freshening wind. She glanced at the sky. There were one or two mares' tails forming against the blue, presaging the rain that the milkman had already forecast.

'I wonder if I ought to go back for my mac?' she murmured. She was not too far away from the house yet, and Reeve and Willy had been going out, would probably already be on their way. She looked round for the dog.

'Gyp, wait for me!' she called to him sharply. To her dismay the animal was already half way up the fellside, his speed belying his age. Scattered bunches of sheep lay in his path, and a sharp stab of fear shot through her. She forgot her mac, and Reeve, everything but the dog, and Ben's dour warning. 'Wait for me!' she cried, and hurried upwards as fast as the steep incline would allow. Gyp waited for her. With docile indifference he stood and allowed her to catch up, and remained close to her when she started off again. That was one advantage of having an ex-sheep-dog, she thought thankfully, they were accustomed to instant obedience, and the habits of a lifetime remained.

'We'll go as far as the waterfall, and then turn back,' she told him. It was pointless to return for her mac now, if she carried on she could be back at the Fleece long before the rain came. Determinedly she gave herself up to the enjoyment of the walk. It was good to be moving, it helped to calm her mind, and in some measure at least to blot out the tensions of the night before. It was necessary to keep moving, she realised, as she climbed higher. The wind had a keen bite to it that pentrated her sweater and slacks with a coolness that was welcome now, while she was on the move, but would rapidly become uncomfortable if she stayed still for long. There was no sign of Ben on the hill, and for that she was grateful. She did not feel she could endure any more of Ben's company for the time being.

The sound of the fall when she reached it made a musical background to the murmurous life of the hill, a low-tuned combination of creature activity that enhanced, rather than broke, the silence, and she leaned against a boulder to watch the tumbling waters and rest for a moment before turning back. Gyp flopped beside her, panting, his upsurge of energy temporarily spent. Perhaps she was worrying unnecessarily. The dog did not *have* to turn rogue, simply because Ben suggested it. She let her eyes drift lazily upwards, her artist's senses appreciating the weather-sculptured forms of the scattered rocks that followed the line of the fall. Something white moved among the higher ones, close to where she had rested when Reeve came to her, but on the edge of the actual drop of the fall. It moved again, and her attention sharpened.

'I must know what it is.' She jumped to her feet, her vitality restored by curiosity. She picked her way carefully upwards among the tumbled rocks. Whatever it was, it was right over the edge of the fall.

'Why, it's my handkerchief! The one I dropped.' The one she could not stop to pick up because Reeve held her, forcing her to go with him towards the helicopter. Now was her chance to retrieve it. A quick smile touched her lips. So much for Reeve's arrogance! She would get her handkerchief back despite him. 'It's a bit far out....' She paused and eyed it cautiously. The rocks were loose on the edge of the waterfall, and it would behove her to be careful. The wind had blown the lace-edged square on to the twigs of a stunted bush growing out of the thin surface soil, and overhanging the fall.

'I can just reach it, I think.'

She climbed down carefully, and she might have succeeded in retrieving it if the rock beneath her feet had remained stable. She stretched her arm over the void, her fingers within an inch of her quarry—half an inch—a quarter—and the sideways pressure of her foot upon the piece of rock proved too much for the gravity exerted by its weight. Just as she grasped the lace border of her handkerchief, the beleagured stone rolled. An agonising pain shot through her ankle, she just had time to wonder if it was broken, when an empty space of rushing water and nothingness raced towards her. She dropped the handkerchief. She did not see this time where it went, and there was no time to care.

Her frantically grasping fingers found sharp rock, grabbed and held on, the roughness of it lacerating her skin until the pain in her hands rivalled that in her ankle, but she held on grimly. She dared not let go. She glanced down and hurriedly averted her eyes. Her body dangled over the edge of the fall and her feet scrabbled desperately to find a hold. Her damaged foot found one, but the pain when she put pressure on it was more than she could bear. For a second she felt her senses swim, and she exerted all her willpower to hold on to consciousness. At all costs she must not faint. It could cost her her life.

Fear caught at her with icy fingers, that nevertheless had the effect of restoring her failing senses. If she could pull herself a little higher, she could edge her whole body on to a bigger slab of rock just above and to the right of her, and gain enough security to rest for a while until the pain in her ankle eased and she could decide what best to do next. Cautiously she felt round with the toe of her other shoe, seeking a foothold. The rocks at the side of the fall were slimy with spray, and her foot slipped, adding to the strain on the twin agonies that were her hands. The second foothold gave her more purchase, and taking a deep gulp of air she began to ease herself upwards.

If the rough point of rock she held on to behaved in the same manner as the stone she had stood on.... For a second or two, the possibility terrorised her into frozen immobility, and she blinked to clear her suddenly blurred gaze, but even her fear-sharpened vision could detect no flaw in the granite under her hands. She inspected it closely, and found it was as grey, and as solid—as rock! Her forehead felt damp, and she rested it for a moment or two against her sleeve, rubbing it clear. The familiar feel of the soft wool had a comforting effect, and it gave her the courage to seek another foothold. Briefly she swung by her hands again, but this time it was deliberate, and controlled, and within a few seconds her cautious seeking found another toe hold higher up.

'I shouldn't have panicked,' she derided her very natural reaction scornfully. 'It's easy enough, if I keep calm.'

It was the reverse of easy, but her years of travelling and self-reliance stood her in good stead now, and she kept her eyes on her goal and inched herself slowly upwards, and to the right, deliberately stopping now and then to rest, until with a final supreme effort she pulled herself up on to the flat slab of rock that lay back for a couple of feet into the hillside, and offered a haven where she could rest for a while before continuing her still not inconsiderable journey to the top, and safety.

She rolled over on to her face, almost sobbing in her thankfulness to have reached this far. The slab was cold under her, damp from the spray of the fall, and sunless in the enclosing narrow confines of rock, and she shivered and got slowly to her knees. She must not remain here for too long, the cold would stiffen her limbs and make climbing out even more hazardous. She glanced upwards, and realised with a thrill of horror that there was no way she could climb out from where she stood. She had been so intent on reaching safety that she had not noticed she was climbing into a trap.

A rocky overhang sloped out over her head like a roof. It blotted out her view of the sky as effectively as it would

hide her from the sight of anyone walking on the fell
above her. As effectively as the sound of her voice calling
for help would be drowned by the constant roar of the
waterfall.

'Reeve!'

She knew he could not hear her but she called just the
same. His name fell instinctively from her trembling lips,
a desperate plea for help that her numbed mind felt only
he could give.

'Reeve!'

She heard Gyp whine. The high, sharp sound penetrated the roar of the water, her only link with the warm,
safe world outside. And then there was only the noise of
the fall. Although she called, twice, the dog did not give
tongue again. In spite of her own predicament Marion
wondered uneasily what Gyp was doing. Would he get
bored when she did not appear, and go home? Perhaps
relieve his boredom on the way by harrying a few sheep?
She knew he had only to taste the undisciplined excitement once, to be irretrievably lost.

She shivered. The cold was intense. It seeped through
her thin sweater and slacks, and she regretted her forgotten
mac. That, at least, would have helped keep the cold at
bay for a little longer. She already felt numb, her power
to think escaping her with the need to keep warm. And
she had to think, to keep her wits about her. To extricate
herself, she would have to climb down again, and then up.
Straight up, not veering to the right as she had done
before. Would her foot stand it? The pain seemed almost
to have disappeared. She shivered again. Before she dared
another climb she must get warm somehow. Frozen hands
and feet would not support her, they could not feel for
holds on the slippery rock. She gathered herself together
and started to jump up and down—and gave an agonised
cry as she came down heavily on her damaged ankle.

Pain pierced her—unbearable pain. And on its
heels a blanket of darkness descended, and the sound of the
waterfall became muted in her ears. She could feel the cold

dampness of the rock through the thin wool of her sweater. Why was she lying on the rock? She had got up, once.... Her last conscious thought was of Reeve. She would never see him again. The icy coldness of the rock should have stopped that from hurting, but it seemed to have no power to anaesthetise that kind of pain. He would never know she loved him.... The blanket of darkness folded right round her, and she settled into its embrace with a sigh, letting it blot out the cold, and the noise of the water, and even the thought of Reeve.

Another sound gradually pierced through the noise of the water. It seemed to come from a long way off. The falls seemed louder now, and someone must have taken away the dark blanket, because she became conscious of cold. Freezing cold, that was too intense even for her to shiver. She opened her eyes and gazed outwards, blankly.

'Marion!'

Someone was calling her name. The sound of it echoed even above the roar of the waterfall. Strong, confident—and urgent.

'Marion!'

It was Reeve's voice. She must be dreaming—or light-headed. But surely it was heat that made people delirious, not cold? She rubbed her eyes, trying to see through the haze that the darkness had left behind. There seemed to be something solid hanging against the white ribbon of the falling water. A disembodied darkness, that descended against the foaming spray, hovering without any kind of support. She watched it come down slowly, with detached interest. Surely only birds could hover? Perhaps it was just a shadow against the falling water. The shadow of an eagle?

'Marion!'

It was no shadow. She tried ineffectively to struggle upright, but the effort defeated her and she slumped back on the rock. It was the eagle himself. Now she knew she was lightheaded. But it did not seem to matter any more. Nothing mattered but that Reeve had come to her. He swung gently towards her and back again, like a pendulum, then he came towards her again and his feet touched the rock on which she lay. He reached out strong hands and grasped a projection, holding himself upright, and with one quick step he stood over her.

The eagle had come home to his eyrie. But not to his mate. More like, she thought confusedly, to his prey. She gazed up at him helplessly, still unable to believe the truth her eyes conveyed. He seemed to have some sort of harness strapped round him; vaguely she noticed one of the heavy buckles shone dully in the shadowed hollow of the cliff. She kept her eyes on the shine, willing it to remain there, not to go away. For what seemed an endless minute Reeve remained upright, staring down at her with his piercing, hooded eyes, then he bent, and she felt his arms go round her, his voice speak to her. He spoke twice before the wonderful truth penetrated her numbed mind. He was not an hallucination, he was real. He was actually there. The cold, and the danger, and the fear paled into insignificance because Reeve was there.

'Are you hurt much?'

'My ankle.' Her face felt so stiff with cold that she could hardly speak.

'Nowhere else?'

She shook her head dumbly. Her head did not count as an injury. Gently he leaned down and eased her up until she rested against his shoulder, then he put his arms under her and lifted her high, away from the cold, damp rock, and his touch galvanised her back to life. The warmth of it flowed through her body, bringing co-ordination back to her frozen limbs, consciousness to her numbed mind.

'Hold me close. Don't let me go,' she heard herself whisper.

'You can't fall, I'm going to strap you to me.' He misunderstood her. 'Put your arms around my neck, and hold on if it'll make you feel any safer.'

She was not afraid of falling. The void she feared was not the edge of the waterfall, but the emptiness of living without Reeve's love. Just the same she put her arms round his neck as he wedged himself back against the rock, and thrust up one foot on the other side, making a knee for her to sit on. The hair on the back of his head, cropped practically short, felt soft against her frozen fingers as she clasped them behind his neck, and she longed to run her hands through it, to pull his head close down to her own, and feel again the burning pressure of his lips.

But Reeve was not looking at her; his eyes were intent on something else. She heard the clink of metal on metal, felt his hands fumble about her waist, and then something pulled tight round her middle, binding her body close to his; she could feel the muscular hardness of his frame against her.

'There's no need to be afraid, you can't fall now we're strapped together.'

As if she could be afraid with Reeve, she thought with a detached kind of surprise. Her arms stayed round his neck, clinging, longing.... Surely through their tight hold he must feel the message of her heart, sense all the things it tried to say, and could not utter? He gave the webbing straps an experimental tug, gave a small grunt of satisfaction, then wound his own arms about her, and for an instant her heart beat high with a wild hope, but all he said was,

'Willy's going to winch us both up into the helicopter as soon as I give him the signal. Just lie still, you can't fall while I'm holding you,' he repeated his assurance.

So that was how he had managed to appear down the funnel of the fall, apparently without any kind of support. For the first time she noticed the line attached to the back of his harness. He let go of her for a moment to reach backwards and give it three sharp tugs—his signal to Willy. She stirred uneasily, resenting even the brief loosening of his grip from about her. She wanted both his arms round her, holding her. In the sweet intimacy of their closeness she would tell him she loved him, and then surely all would be well?

'Reeve. . . .'

'Don't talk now. Save telling me what happened until later. We're going up.'

'But I want to tell you. . . .'

She wasn't going to tell him what happened to toss her over the fall. What did that matter? she wondered bemusedly. She had something much more important to say to him. But just as she was about to tell him so, his arm came back round her in a hard, breath-expelling hold. One of his hands pressed her head close against his shoulder, guarding it against the danger of being bumped against the rock as they rose, and at the same time denying her the ability to speak, because her face was pressed against him, and without warning they swung outwards, away from the rocky slab, into nothingness.

She closed her eyes and gave herself up to his arms. She felt his feet fend them off from the rocks on their first pendulum swing, felt the cold wetness of the spray as they closed in on the waterfall, and then out again, steadier now as Willy drew them inexorably upwards. The rim of the waterfall appeared above them, then below them, and she opened her eyes on the homely, familiar face of the fellside, with its sheep, and its heather, and its wonderful, everyday normality. Then why could she still feel the spray from the fall? She raised her face from Reeve's shoulder. The wetness came down round them in an endless cascade as they continued to rise towards the hovering machine, and she realised it was raining. The rain forecast by the milkman's gammy leg, and the mares' tails in the sky when she set out on her walk. She began to laugh weakly, and to cry at the same time. And then she remembered Gyp.

'The dog—he mustn't stay on the fell on his own.'

'He isn't on the fell, he's in here, with me.' Willy's friendly arms reached out to support her as the line drew them both up into the warm, safe cabin of the helicopter. His round face, for once minus its usual cheerful grin, anxiously scanned her own.

'What's the damage, Skipper?' he asked Reeve, and his

voice was taut with concern.

'Shock, cold, and a badly sprained ankle,' Reeve replied tersely. 'Help unbuckle her, will you? My hands are too cold to work properly.' Was it her imagination, or did the ice reach his voice as well?

'Let me rub the circulation back into yours.' Willy took her two small hands in his much larger, blissfully warm ones. 'It's a good job I'd arranged to pick Reeve up on the hill,' he exclaimed, 'you're like a block of ice! My, but you're going to get a bad dose of hot-aches in these before they're useable again.' He turned her hands palm upwards, preparatory to giving them the promised rub, and gave vent to a low whistle of sympathy. 'You have taken a bad tumble, haven't you?' He held them up for Reeve to see.

'They'll dress them at the hospital, and have a look at her ankle at the same time.'

'I don't want to go to hospital.' From somewhere she found enough energy to protest.

'You haven't got any choice,' he told her curtly, and this time there was no mistaking the coldness of his voice. 'I'm taking you there, whether you want to go or not.'

'Mrs Pugh will wonder where I've got to.'

'She won't. I followed you across the fell, I said we'd probably walk back the long way, and be a bit late.'

'You followed me?'

'It's a good job I did,' he ignored the question in her voice. 'When I was half way up the fell I met Gyp, heading for home and help as fast as his old legs would carry him.' He reached down and fondled the dog's grey muzzle, and incredibly Marion felt a sharp stab of jealousy that he should lavish his affection on the dog when she needed it so much more. 'He kicked up such a fuss, trying to herd me towards the waterfall, that I guessed something was wrong and sent him on ahead. He led me straight to the edge of the fall. Even then I might not have realised where you were, except that your handkerchief had got caught up on the twigs of that bush when you fell over.'

'It was trying to get it back that made me fall in the

first place.' Marion spoke without thinking, and she was quite unprepared for the blaze of anger that scorched her as Reeve shouted incredulously,

'Do you mean your handkerchief had blown over the fall, and you actually risked your life to get it back?' She wanted to get it back to checkmate Reeve, but she dared not tell him so in the face of his undisguised fury. 'Have you taken leave of your senses?' he stormed.

'I—it——' She quailed before the anger in his face.

'Not content with creeping out to meet Ben Wade, you had to try to get yourself killed as well!'

'Ben Wade?' What had Ben Wade got to do with it? she wondered, bewildered by the intensity of his attack. 'I wasn't going to meet Ben Wade.'

'Don't lie to me,' he snapped angrily. 'Why else would you walk as far as the waterfall on a wet morning, and without a mac at that, if you weren't in such a hurry to keep an assignation with Ben Wade? I expect you'd arranged between you to set up another protest meeting, the same as the one you organised in the bar-room last night,' he flung at her harshly.

CHAPTER ELEVEN

At least Reeve did not think she had gone courting Ben. It should have given her a small crumb of comfort, but it could not penetrate the shock of his accusing anger.

'Airport coming up.'

Willy's laconic warning cut across the brittle atmosphere between herself and Reeve, and they both turned and automatically looked down. The flying field showed vividly green after the dun-coloured hillside, and the wet tarmac glistened under the rain.

'Put this on,' Reeve commanded her curtly, and handed over a bundle of something darkly coloured. She took it, and saw it was her mac.

'How ... ?'

'I brought it with me when I came up the hill.'

How had he known where she was going in the first place?

'I heard Gyp give tongue in the walled garden,' he answered her unspoken question, and she remembered the chase after the cat. 'I put two and two together,' he added significantly.

And made five, she thought wearily, but she did not argue with him. What was the use? He believed she had gone to meet Ben Wade, and nothing she could say would be likely to alter his opinion. She shrugged into the mac and started to button it round her, winced as her grazed fingers fumbled on the buttons. Reeve turned to her impatiently and pulled her hands away.

'I'll do it,' he told her curtly, 'your fingers are sore enough, without making them worse.' She desisted, and let them lie limply in her lap while he did up the buttons, all six of them, and seemed to take an endless age over the last one. She could feel his fingers brush her chin, and she lifted her head, trying not to let him touch her, because his touch weakened her resolve, and she was dangerously close to tears as it was.

'You won't be out in the rain for long, but there's no sense in getting any wetter than you already are,' his voice criticised the reason for her being wet at all.

'I'll drop the 'copter as close to the car as I can,' Willy said accommodatingly 'you won't have so far to walk then.' In spite of her distress, Marion had to admire the skill that carefully settled the big machine within a few feet of where the Rover stood waiting for them near the airport building.

'I'll go and open the car, I can come back and see to the rotor afterwards.' Willy took the key from Reeve and jumped out of the machine, eagerly followed by the dog, who sensed the prospect of another ride.

'I can walk that far, it's only a few steps.' Marion stiffened as Reeve leaned towards her.

'You'll keep off your foot until we know whether your ankle's broken, or only sprained.' He made it an order, and she flushed resentfully, but she was sitting at the limit of her seat and there was no room to move away; he bent and picked her up as if she was no more than a featherweight in his arms, and swung himself and her out of the helicopter to the car with easy steps, as if he held no burden.

'Front or back, Skipper?' Willy held both doors wide open for choice.

'Front,' Marion's heart cried. 'In the front beside Reeve.'

'Back,' Reeve said briefly, and bending he let her down carefully on to the wide, comfortable back seat, and eased her towards the end of it. 'Lean back and keep your foot up.' He settled a couple of cushions behind her shoulders and head and laid her legs along the length of the car seat. 'You as well,' he snapped his fingers to the dog, and smiled as Gyp jumped in beside her without hesitation. He did not smile at Marion, and her heart mourned the omission. Her hand strayed down to Gyp's silky head, seeking the comfort of his warm, licking tongue and waving tail. The dog seemed to be the only one left who wanted her, she thought drearily. Because of Reeve, the people in the valley would shun her. She had never sought their company before, now she wanted it desperately. Her uncle was buried in his writing, Mrs Pugh immersed in the management of the hotel, and Reeve. . . . Reeve glared at her as if he hated her. She did not count Willy. He was friendly enough, but because of his work he was committed to Reeve and not for anything would she come between them.

'I'll go and tether the 'copter,' Willy spoke to Reeve from outside the car. 'You go on, if you're in a hurry, I'll get back on my own.'

'A few minutes won't make all that much difference,' Reeve told him decisively. 'We'll wait.' He made no effort to get into the car with Marion while they waited. Instead, he shut the back door on her with a finality that dropped her spirits to zero and brought the tears perilously close to the surface. He leaned casually against the hood of the car, thrusting his hands deep into his parka pockets, and seemed impervious himself to the rain. She could see the wet drops glisten on his dark hair, outlining his high forehead and the stern set of his features as he waited patiently while Willy and a mechanic tethered the rotor blade.

She closed her eyes, but the soft sweep of her lashes against her cheeks could not prevent the escape of a tear. It trickled into the dark hollows under her eyes, more pronounced now than when she had got up that morning, and lay there gleaming damply in the subdued light from the rear window, treacherously betraying her inner turmoil to the grey hawk gaze that flicked over her briefly as Reeve took his seat beside Willy in the front and brought it back again to rest on her face with a strange expression that she could not see because she resolutely kept her eyes closed.

'I'll drive.'

She heard him speak to Willy, felt the big car rock slightly as the two men took their seats, and the doors thudded to as the engine purred into life, and the motion told her they were on their way. She did not need the low-toned conversation between Reeve and Willy to tell her which seat Reeve sat in. Nor did she need to open her eyes to see in front of her the broad shoulders, rippling slightly as he moved his arms to manipulate the controls, topped by the strong, tanned column of his neck to where it met the crisp, dark hair, neatly barbered above his collar, and curling slightly into the nape in a way that made her long to run her fingers along the thick, springy line of it. The sheer dynamic force of him reached across the intervening space to touch her, and set her pulses racing.

'Today's a write-off.' It was Reeve speaking. 'I'll have to come out with you for an hour or two tomorrow instead, if we're to make that final survey.'

'We couldn't have seen a lot today anyway, the ceiling's

too low.' Willy resorted to jargon to describe the rain clouds.

'Probably not, but we could have seen some,' Reeve argued. 'As it is, it'll be too late by the time we get back. The light will be too poor.'

He did not mind her knowing she had wasted his day. Marion's eyes flew open, and she sat upright abruptly, and straightaway gave a gasp as she put pressure on the already ill-treated palms of her hands to help her up.

'We thought you'd dropped off to sleep.' Willy caught the slight sound. He turned instantly and smiled at her, and somehow she managed a weak smile back. Reeve knew she had not been asleep, otherwise he would not have made such a remark. She burned with indignation.

'I said I didn't want to go to hospital, in the first place,' she snapped at the back of his head.

'You need to go,' he replied without turning, 'what you want is quite irrelevant,' he added evenly. 'And since we're already here there's little point now in turning back.' He swung the Rover through a pair of open iron gates and drew up smoothly in front of a red brick annexe to a tall, grey stone building, over which a foot-high sign declared it to be the Casualty Department entrance.

'I'll walk.'

This time she was determined he would not carry her—she refused to be beholden to him again. If she was quick, she could slide out feet first on the other side of the car the moment Willy opened the back door. The pilot swung out of his seat, and she waited impatiently for her escape route to appear. Willy put his hand on the door handle. She did not hear the door open against her back. The first she knew of it was a draught of cool air against her neck, then Reeve reached in and put his one arm round her waist and pulled her backwards along the seat towards him. She started violently at his unexpected touch, but he kept hold of her and kept on pulling. She could not struggle. He held her too tightly for her to offer any serious resistance, and in seconds she was hanging in his hold, suspended over the tarmac of the hospital drive, but before her feet could leave the car seat after her body Reeve's other arm came up under her knees, and he lifted her high against him.

'Put me down!' she whispered furiously. 'I don't want your help.'

'I told you,' he tightened his grip, 'what you want is irrelevant.'

What she really wanted was irrelevant to him, she thought unhappily, and it hurt worse than her ankle and her two hands put together. She moved restlessly, and his voice hardened.

'If you don't lie still, I'll....'

'Would you like a wheelchair for the lady, sir?' What Reeve intended to do was lost to her by the appearance of a friendly hospital porter, with an offer of help, which to her chagrin Reeve instantly refused.

'I can manage, she's not heavy,' he said firmly. 'Where to?' he asked.

'This way, sir, the room on the left.' Without another word Reeve carried her over to the couch the porter indicated, and deposited her in the middle of the blankets. 'Now if you'll wait outside?' The man ushered Reeve away. 'We won't keep you apart any longer than we can help,' he told Marion with what was meant to be a kindly smile. She grimaced as he drew the curtains round the couch. If he did but know it, he was doing her a favour by separating them, she thought angrily.

'Hold your breath, this will sting.' The young doctor who appeared was brisk and efficient, and unfortunately truthful. Whatever it was he soaked the cotton wool with to clean her hands felt like hot coals on her lacerated palms. 'It'll soon pass.' Fortunately his comforting words were accurate as well, and no sooner had her involuntary gasp of agony receded than her hands began to feel surprisingly comfortable. He bandaged on a light padding and turned his attention to her ankle. 'There isn't any break.' He slipped the X-ray plates into a wallclip and switched on the light behind them. 'Not even a crack,' he confirmed. 'It's just a bad strain. Painful, but nuisance value only.' He had his own priorities, Marion realised, but the thought of being rendered immobile filled her with dismay. It could not have come at a more inconvenient time.

'Shall I be able to use it at all?' she asked anxiously.

'I shouldn't, not for a couple of days, until the worst of the swelling has gone down,' her white-coated companion advised. 'I'll strap it up for you.' He proceeded to do so with dexterous fingers, and chancing to look up, caught the expression of consternation on her face. His own broke into a reassuring smile. 'Don't worry, we'll make you mobile,' he promised. 'Try these.' He took a pair of crutches the porter handed through the curtains, and watched her critically as she experimented with a step or two. 'You should manage nicely on those,' he encouraged, then rolled aside the cubicle curtains and walked with her back to where Reeve sat outside. He rose as soon as they appeared and came towards them, and the doctor spoke directly to him.

'Bring her back the day after tomorrow,' he suggested. 'The swelling should have subsided by then, and in the meantime, having the crutches will lessen the inconvenience.'

And effectively prevent Reeve from picking her up again, Marion thought with satisfaction. She could not resist a small, triumphant glance in his direction, but his face was expressionless, and his grey eyes returned her look with an inscrutable stare. He walked with her slowly towards the car, adjusting his pace to hers and the porter walked on her other side.

'Like jailers,' she thought with an ill-timed desire to giggle, that she hastily suppressed. It was not a particularly funny ending to her ill-starred walk with the dog, and but for Reeve it could have been tragic. The thought sobered her, and she concentrated on mastering her new aids, thankful for the soft padding bandaged to her palms that eased the pressure against the cross bars of the crutches. At least she would be able to get about without too much trouble.

'I can manage to get in on my own.'

She spoke with defiant dignity as they reached the car, and wordlessly Reeve opened the door for her—the front passenger door, not the back one this time. She gave him a startled look, but he held out his hands for her crutches, and she gave them to him in silence. She would have preferred to do without his help altogether, her look told him so, but she could not get into the car and hold the crutches at the same time. He waited patiently enough as she settled comfortably into the seat, and he had shut the door on her before she realised he still had the crutches in his hand.

'I'll take them. . . .'

She turned to open the door again, and then it dawned on her that even the roomy interior of the front passenger compartment was not designed to take long, inflexible rods of wood without discomfort to the person who sat in the seat. Did Reeve know this when he deliberately put her in the front? Perhaps hoping to make things more awkward for her, by depriving her of the one thing that ensured her independence of him? she wondered angrily. She heard the back door of the car open behind her, but she resolutely refused to look round. Probably he intended to put the crutches along the length of the back seat, but she determined she would not give him the satisfaction of knowing his action had disconcerted her. She heard him snap his fingers to Gyp, and the dog jump eagerly into the rear well, then Willy said,

'Ready to go, Skipper?'

She averted her eyes as Reeve nodded an affirmative, and turned towards the hospital porter, no doubt to thank him for his help, then he was climbing into the car beside her, easing his long length under the wheel, his hands reaching for the controls.

She ought to have thanked the porter herself. Guiltily she turned to look out of the side window, and pinned on a bright smile she was far from feeling, to serve as her own display of gratitude. Impulsively she raised her hand to wave to the porter, then it dropped limply back into her lap, and her smile faded as she saw what it was the man held in his hands.

Her pair of crutches.

'You've given him back the crutches! You've no right....' She turned to stare incredulously from the porter to Reeve. 'Stop the car! At once!' she demanded, as he set the vehicle rolling, and showed no signs of hearing, let alone obeying her. 'You know I can't walk without them for at least two days,' she stormed angrily.

'The less you're able to walk about, the less mischief you can get into,' he replied grimly. He raised his hand in a courteous salute to the porter, smiled as it was returned —gleefully, Marion saw, because his underhand ploy had succeded so well—then swung the big car out of the hospital gates, and eased it skilfully into the fast-moving traffic streaming along the main road.

'You're trying to stop me from moving about so that I shan't be able to do anything about your wretched reservoir plan,' she flashed at him accusingly. The slick ease with which he had accomplished his object choked her with fury.

'Let's say I prefer to know where you are at any given time.' Reeve slanted a sideways glance at her, and her feelings boiled over as his lips quirked upwards in a grin. He was laughing at her! Enjoying her defeat....

'You—you——' She glared at him in impotent fury. She longed to strike the clean-cut, laughing lips. The desire to do so was almost irresistible. Her hand actually rose again, and then the sharp clang of an ambulance bell heading urgently towards the hospital entrance cooled her fury as effectively as a cold shower. Reeve was driving. If she struck him it would distract his attention from the road, perhaps make the car swerve. For an appalling moment she felt she did not care, so long as it was only Reeve who was hurt. Then the moment passed, and left

her cold and trembling, shaken to the core by her glimpse
of what deeply stirred emotions could do to a normally
gentle nature, and sickened that it was she—Marion—
who had, if only for a few brief seconds, so loathed a fellow
human being.

She lay back in her seat, drained by the force of the
spent emotion, the depths of which she had never experienced before, and had no wish to do so again. But
then, she had never loved before, either, and it was said
that love and hate were akin. And now she knew both,
intimately. From a long way off she heard Willy speak
from the back of the car.

'If the cloud clears, we can go up again tomorrow, or the
day after.'

'It'll have to be tomorrow. I'm bringing Marion back to
the hospital the day after.'

'You needn't put yourself out on my account,' she
told him sharply. 'Today's already been a write-off because
of me,' she flung his own words back at him bitingly. 'I
wouldn't dream of troubling you again. I can get a taxi.'
For a brief, traitorous moment, she almost wished they
lived in Merevale, where there was a bus service.

'It needn't be a trouble,' he assured her smoothly. 'The
trip to the hospital shouldn't take very long, and afterwards
we could go and have some lunch, and come back at our
leisure during the afternoon.'

'Lunch, as well as the trip into Dale End?' She looked
at him in amazement. 'What a waste of time,' she jeered.
'Think of all the work you could be doing instead. All the
people you could be interviewing—no, bribing—to leave
their homes,' she corrected herself sarcastically.

'Well, isn't that what you want?' he asked her. He
slanted a glance at her, cold, probing, and distinctly hostile.

'What, for you to take me back to the hospital?' That was
the last thing she wanted, she told herself.

'No, for you to take me away from my work.' His
mimicry brought an angry flush to her cheeks. 'It's an
ideal delaying tactic,' he pressed his point home remorse-

lessly. 'You'll gain at least another twenty-four hours, possibly more if the cloud continues low, and I still can't finish the survey I should have done this morning.'

'If you're suggesting I fell over the waterfall simply to foil your plans——' she began hotly.

'I'm suggesting nothing of the kind,' he said smoothly, and drew to a halt on the forecourt of the Fleece. He slid out of his seat and came round to her side of the car, and with calm deliberation he opened the door and reached in, and picked her up in his arms. 'You can't walk without your crutches, remember,' he grinned, and she willed herself to remain still, to appear indifferent. His face—his lips—were close above her own, too close for her peace of mind, and she hastily turned her face into his sweater so that she need not look up and meet his eyes. If she did, she feared the expression in her own might betray her.

'It's an excellent delaying tactic,' he goaded her, reverting to his earlier remark.

'The same sort of tactic that you used to alienate me from everyone else in the bar-room?' she flung back bitterly, anger restoring her courage. Strategically, his tactics had been remarkably successful, but he was well versed in their use, and she was not.

'The same sort of thing,' he agreed unabashed. 'If there's going to be a fight,' he continued, his voice challenging, 'then let battle commence, with no holds barred, and no quarter given on either side,' he warned her.

CHAPTER TWELVE

SHE deliberately got up late the next morning, to avoid seeing Reeve. She made her foot the excuse, although there was no need, she saw with relief; the combination of firm bandaging and a night's rest had reduced the swelling to negligible proportions. She tried it cautiously, and found with the support of the bandage she could even stand on it without too much discomfort.

'Have your breakfast in bed for a change. A rest won't do you any harm.'

She took the tray Mrs Pugh brought up to her and started on the contents with a pang of conscience. Her injuries did not warrant breakfast in bed, but to please the housekeeper she ate what she was given without demur, and gave the empty tray to Rose who popped an enquiring head round her door to see if she was awake.

'I'm getting up,' she announced, 'it's only grazed hands and a sprained ankle. Those won't stop me from working on my woodcut.'

She slipped into a fresh sweater and slacks. Those she had on the day before looked very much the worse for wear, she decided ruefully. The chocolate brown outfit had been one of her favourites, but it had suffered from her unpleasant experience almost as much as she had. She searched out a chunky cream sweater and some new red corduroys, and added a heavy garnet pendant for good measure. The bright splash of colour raised her spirits miraculously, and her mirror boosted her confidence enough to send her downstairs feeling more cheerful than when she had ascended them the night before.

'The clouds are still low,' she commented to Rose, who was busy with duster and polish on the landing. The air felt cool, and she glanced out of the landing window. Reeve would not be able to work from the helicopter today. The ceiling, as Willy called it, was still very low, she saw with malicious satisfaction.

'Has Mr Harland gone out yet?' she asked Rose casually. She had slept soundly after her experiences, and did not hear him get up or go downstairs.

'I haven't seen him, miss. Oh, perhaps that's him now. Did you want him?' Rose got ready to run and fetch him as the front door slammed on an unseen back, and receding footsteps echoed on the forecourt outside.

'No, don't disturb him, it'll do later,' Marion checked her

hurriedly, and waited until she heard an engine start and a car drive away. It was safe for her to go downstairs at last.

'I shouldn't walk too far on that ankle,' Rose warned her, and she smiled.

'I won't.' She was too keenly aware of the possible consequences if she was rash enough to ignore the doctor's advice, and she had no desire to be incapacitated for any longer than was absolutely necessary. As it was, her injury would prevent her from doing much for a few days to keep a check on Reeve's moves among the inhabitants of Fallbeck, and perhaps assuage some of the damage his persuasive tongue might inflict, she thought grimly. It only needed one family to give in, and agree to leave.... The thought sent her downstairs one step at a time, on her seat instead of her feet. She could hop the rest of the way through the kitchen to the stable block, she decided. She reached the bottom with a feeling of achievement when Reeve strolled along the passage and halted in front of her.

'Where are you off to?' he enquired interestedly.

'I thought you'd gone out. The door slammed....'

She went scarlet with mortification. After taking all that trouble to avoid Reeve, and now she had to blurt that out. He would guess she had been waiting for him to go out, before coming downstairs. The gleam in his eyes told her he knew, and that it amused him.

'That was Willy,' he informed her. 'He treats every door as if it was fixed to his helicopter cabin.'

'I'm going to my studio.' She stood up and hoped fervently she would be able to walk without a limp. For the first time she deliberately called it a studio, and bit her lip as she saw his twitch. That seemed to amuse him, too.

'Allow me.' He picked her up without ado, and her patience snapped.

'For goodness' sake, put me down!' she shouted angrily.

'For your ankle's sake—no!' he refused her calmly, and tightened his hold.

'Willy will be waiting for you.' She tried another tactic. Why did he have to cradle her so tenderly against his heart that she could feel it beating next to her own? Did he do it deliberately, because he knew how it undermined her resistance to him?

'Willy's gone to prepare the helicopter....'

'You won't be able to fly today, the cloud's too low.' She did not try to hide the satisfaction in her voice, and his eyes gleamed. The light of battle, perhaps? The battle in which no holds were barred? The hold he had on her now was one she would not try to bar, if only it meant the same to him as it did to her.

'... to prepare the helicopter for when the cloud lifts,' he finished his interrupted sentence, and grinned as he saw her face fall. 'In the meantime,' he toed open the door of her studio and deposited her carefully on her stool in front of her neglected woodcut, 'in the meantime,' he said significantly, 'I've got several people to see, to start negotiations with regard to their properties, so the time won't be wasted.' He stressed 'negotiations'. Marion had called it bribery.

'Who are the people you're going to try to bribe?' she corrected his definition bitingly, and had the satisfaction of seeing his face tighten.

'Do you expect me to tell you that?' He shook his head, and the light in his eyes became steely. 'If I told you, I'd be playing right into the hands of the opposition,' he refused her. 'I didn't go to the trouble of spiking your guns,' he referred to his effective disposal of the crutches, 'merely to give you any information you ask for, like a naïve schoolboy. Oh, by the way,' he turned at the door and came back towards her, 'here's your chisel.' He slid a long, narrow wrapped package on to her work bench. 'Don't drop it on the floor again,' he said critically, 'it's too fine a tool to be damaged by carelessness.'

And then he was gone. Briefly his figure blocked the

doorway, shutting out the light from her work bench. With a decisive click he shut the half door behind him. The click stirred her into action. Even Reeve would not have the effrontery to lock her in—would he? In her haste to get to the door, she forgot her damaged ankle, and it reminded her sharply that it still expected to be treated with consideration. She gave a gasp and held on to the stool for support, and nearly dropped the chisel again. She grabbed and caught it, and gave a sigh of relief as she managed to prevent it from landing on the quarries for the second time. Not that she cared two cents for Reeve's warning, she told herself wrathfully. It was only that she, too, had a reverence for good tools. It was about the only thing she and Reeve shared.

She laid the still wrapped chisel safely on the bench and hopped to the door with as much speed as she could muster. The converted stable still retained its half doors. The top half was pegged back permanently against the wall, but the bottom half.... With fingers that shook she pulled it towards her. And almost fell over when it gave easily and swung inwards to her touch.

'I don't need to lock you in.'

Reeve had nearly reached the end of the yard, but he must have heard her and guessed why she was at the door, because he turned.

'Your sprained ankle will serve as an effective ball and chain,' he taunted, and with a derisive wave of his hand he strode out of sight.

She stared at his retreating back in helpless frustration. Even after he turned the corner of the buildings and disappeared, she still gazed at the spot where he vanished, until her one leg began to ache with the strain of supporting her full weight, and she turned and hopped disconsolately back to the stool.

She sat down and passed a hand over her eyes, trying to ease the ache that lay behind them. There was a corresponding ache in her throat, and she swallowed and blinked, then picked up the chisel, resolutely concentrating on unwrapping the oiled paper from around it. As her eyes cleared she looked at the wrapping with closer attention, and noticed it bore the name of a firm of hardware specialists in Dale End, who offered a service to their customers to sharpen any tool from a ploughshare to a penknife. When she dropped the chisel, the iron-hard quarries of the stable floor had chipped the blade. Now there was no chip to be seen. She examined it closely. It had been expertly honed, and—she ran the ball of her thumb gingerly across the edge of the blade—it was razor-sharp. As sharp as Reeve's parting thrust, which brought the ache to her throat, and behind her eyes. He must have taken the chisel in to Dale End specially to get it sharpened for her. She should have been grateful, but. . . .

'I wish he hadn't bothered,' she muttered rebelliously. It was Reeve's fault the blade was damaged in the first place. If he had not startled her, she would not have dropped it. She regarded her favourite tool with distaste. If only she had another one, of the same size. . . . But like her pencil, there was just the one, and she needed it for the finer points of her woodcut.

She turned to her neglected work. The blade of the chisel cut easily, without requiring much pressure from her hands. She still retained the padding on her palms to absorb the thrust of her tool handle, but the keen blade sliced with an ease and precision that in spite of herself filled Marion with the pleasurable satisfaction she always experienced in her work. She soon became completely absorbed, to the exclusion of Reeve and the reservoir, and even her damaged ankle, and the time passed by without her noticing. The clump of carved harebells grew steadily, standing out in bold relief from the base panel, as dainty and lifelike as the sketch which she had pinned on the baize-covered board which stood propped at the back of her bench for guidance.

'Hmmm!'

It could not be Reeve come back. He was not given to apologetic coughs. With his normal arrogant assurance, he

would have walked straight in without an 'excuse me',
she thought tartly. She straightened up reluctantly from her
work. It could not be Willy, either. He had gone to the
airport to service the helicopter.

'Why, Mr Cornish,' she regarded the elderly schoolteacher with surprise, 'what brings you here during school
hours?'

'It's half term.' John Cornish took her smile of welcome
as an invitation, and let himself in through the door. 'I'm
looking for Mr Harland,' he explained. 'Mrs Pugh said he
might still be here with you.'

'He went off a little while ago.' Marion's lips thinned
at the mention of Reeve's name. 'He said he'd got some
calls to make on people. To begin what he calls negotiations for the sale of their property,' she explained, 'and
I'm stuck here with a sprained ankle, and can't do a thing
about it,' she added bitterly.

'Didn't they give you some crutches or something, to
get about on?'

'Yes, but we accidentally left them at the hospital, and
now I'm tied by the heels—literally.' Not for anything
would she admit, even to John Cornish, how easily Reeve
had outwitted her. 'I'll tell Mr Harland you want him,
when he comes back,' she offered.

'I don't particularly want him,' the schoolteacher corrected her wryly, 'but I must see him.'

'About the school?' she queried sympathetically.

'That, and my job.' He looked desperately worried, and
anger surged through Marion anew. Multiplied, the schoolmaster's plight was the plight of everyone in the valley,
thanks to Reeve.

'I envy you,' her companion said wistfully, and at her
enquiring look, 'You can work from wherever you happen
to be.' He ran his fingers appreciatively over her carving.

'But surely, even if the village school closes, you'll be
found a job somewhere else?'

'Of sorts, perhaps,' John Cornish admitted unhappily.
'But I'd hoped to remain here. I've less than two years to

go before I can retire, and it's a bit late to pull up my roots now and start again.'

'I thought the Education Committee were talking about closing the village school anyway, because of lack of pupils?' Marion stopped abruptly. I'm doing Reeve's work for him, saying things like that, she thought with alarm.

'They were, but because I'd got such a short while to retirement, they were biased in favour of keeping the school open until I actually retire at the end of next year. If this valley project goes ahead, it'll tip the scales the other way, and they'll close it anyway. If they do, I'll have to find another teaching post somehow because of my pension. And that won't be easy, at my age.'

'Haven't you got any thought for what you're doing to him? To all of us?' Marion cried when Reeve returned, and she told him John Cornish had called in search of him. 'Don't you care?' She hammered balled fists against his chest, trying to reach the human being that must—had got to, she thought despairingly—lurk somewhere beneath the uncaring outer shell of the reservoir builder. 'Don't you care?'

'If ever I'm in trouble,' he observed whimsically, without answering her question, 'I hope someone will take up the cudgels as fervently on my behalf.'

He caught her fists easily, stilling their urgent beat, and turned her towards him. He had come back to the studio and walked in without asking, just as she knew he would, she told herself caustically, and tried to ignore the small voice that asked her, with maddening persistence, why then had she remained in the studio, when she knew he would return there? Was it because, knowing he would come, she wanted to be there when he did?

'No!' she denied stoutly.

'No?' the voice jeered in silent disbelief.

But Reeve had come, just the same. She was standing back away from her bench, studying the woodcut, when he walked through the door. His gaze swept over her work, over the chisel lying on the bench, and the shavings curled

about the floor, which told him she had been using the tool
he had sharpened for her.

'At least go and see John Cornish, and ease his mind.'
She had not meant to plead with Reeve. The memory of
the elderly schoolmaster's haunted eyes drove her to it,
but it galled her just the same.

'Nothing I can say to John Cornish at the moment is
likely to ease his mind,' he disillusioned her bluntly.

'You went to see the others.'

'Some of them.' Still he did not say which ones, and
Marion stiffened resentfully. 'I made excellent progress,
too,' he goaded her, and her eyes flashed.

'I'll find out who you went to see,' she cried defiantly.
'And what you said to them. What you made them agree
to.'

'I didn't make them agree to anything.' His face hardened.
'I put the facts to them, that's all, and left them to decide
for themselves.'

'Decide whether to take your bribe, or try to make you
pay more.'

Her shot found its mark. She saw his face go white, and
a small muscle at the point of his jaw started to twitch
spasmodically.

'You won't get away with this,' she vowed, 'I won't let
you. I'll phone round and find out who you went to see,
and I'll make whatever you said to them public knowledge.
If everyone knows what's going on, individuals won't be
so inclined to give in to you.' She did not care if he knew
what her plans were, he would find out soon enough what
she intended to do, anyway. 'You've managed to stop me
from walking about for the moment,' she conceded grimly,
'but you can't stop me from talking,' she finished defiantly.

'Can't I?' The silky softness of his tone should have
warned her, but she was too incensed to notice. She rushed
on confidently.

'No, you can't. There's no way you can. . . .'

He showed her the way.

With a quick twist of his hand behind her head, he

turned her face up towards his own, and his lips descended
on hers with punishing force. They drove the words back
into her throat and drove her breath back with them. She
gave a tiny whimper, a small, thin thread of sound, and he
silenced that, too. Her lips parted beneath the pressure of
his kiss, but no words came through them. Their tender
lines lay bruised and silent under the searing force of his
anger. She tried to struggle free, but he held her tightly
against him, her hands trapped against his chest, with
neither the leverage nor the strength to push him away.

Nor the will? The seconds passed, and still his lips
clung to her own, drowning her resistance, as well as her
words, as effectively as he wanted to drown the valley to
make his reservoir. Despairingly she felt her resolve begin
to slip, the armour of her anger melt under the passionate
upsurge of her love which he drew unerringly to the surface
with the fire of his kiss.

She forgot family ties, and the ties of loyalty that bound
her to the valley. The latter were tenuous anyway, despite
her protestations, and with Reeve's arms round her, Reeve's
lips searching her own, she discovered how frail they
really were. There was only Reeve. Nothing else mattered
in the world but him. He could have his reservoir, take the
valley if he wished, if only he would take her, too.

She gave a small moan of surrender, and her body
melted against his, suppliant, weak. His hold on her relaxed
its rigid tightness, freeing her hands, and her arms rose
and clasped him hungrily about his neck, her willing lips
returning kiss for kiss.

'I love you. I love you,' she whispered.

Would he say he loved her, too? Her eyes beseeched him.
They searched his face, and incredibly they found no
softening there. It was set and hard above her, unyielding
in its expression, except for a cynical twist about his lips
that was not even the beginning of a smile. She stared up
at him, nonplussed. The same cynicism was repeated in his
eyes. They looked down at her with angry awareness, and
—yes, she was not mistaken—bitter contempt. The twist

to his lips became more pronounced. She shivered. It was more of a snarl than a smile. He released her, and reaching behind him he tore her hands from behind his head and thrust them back at her with a force that said he loathed the feel of them against him.

'I know I said no holds barred,' his voice cut like a whip, 'but your methods are contemptible,' he gritted.

'My—methods?' She stared at him in stunned incomprehension.

'You don't think I was taken in by that pretty display, do you?' he sneered. 'It was good acting, Marion—but not good enough.' His eyes were like twin pools of ice, and she flinched away from the scorn in his voice.

'You can't get round me in that manner,' he told her roughly. 'I'm not that gullible.' He thrust her away from him, and turned on his heel towards the door. 'Save your wiles for someone naïve enough to be taken in by them,' he threw at her over his shoulder, and kicked open the door with an impatient toe. 'Ben Wade, for example,' he added, and vanished from her sight.

CHAPTER THIRTEEN

REEVE took her to the hospital the next morning, exactly as he promised to. She did not want him to. She dreaded meeting him again. She had not spoken to him since he walked out of her studio the day before. He went out after lunch, she knew that. She hopped over to her bedroom window when she heard his car start up, and saw him draw it out of the garage, and park it in the stable yard.

'He must be waiting for Willy.'

She was safe from observation unless he looked up straight at her window, and he showed not the least inclination to do so, and she watched as he parked the car then got out of it and leaned easily against the hood. It was unusual for Willy to keep him waiting. And to be fair, Reeve did not keep the pilot waiting either, as a rule; there seemed to be a mutual liking and respect between the two men that ironed out any difference there might be in their status.

'Whatever's going on?'

Marion echoed Mrs Pugh's words to herself as a sudden burst of conversation came through the open top of her window, and she looked further across the yard in time to see a group of women appear round the buildings. Three—no, four, another woman hurried to catch up with the others—and Reeve straightened up from the car hood with a courteous greeting, echoed cheerfully by the newcomers. He seemed to be on good terms with them all. Marion's lips curled. No doubt he found it paid to ingratiate himself with them, she thought scornfully.

Her eyebrows raised as Reeve opened the doors and began to usher them into the car. Three in the back, he closed the door carefully behind them, and opened the door to the front passenger seat. Her seat, when she came back from the hospital, next to Reeve.

'I wonder . . .?'

She recognised all the women. They all came from the valley. Two of them were the mothers of the two sets of twins soon due to go to school in Dale End. Her forehead creased in a puzzled frown. Far from scattering the herd, Reeve appeared to be intent on gathering them together.

He shut the door on the last of his passengers and hurried round to the other side of the car and pulled open the driving door. So he was going to be his own chauffeur as well? Marion's curiosity increased, and she took a small step forward, nearer to the window.

Whether it was the movement that attracted his attention, or some process of thought transference, she could not tell. But in the act of stepping into the car, his left foot and leg already inside, out of sight, Reeve twisted round and looked up, straight at her. Could he actually see her? Or did he only guess she was there? There were net curtains at the window, but his eyes bored directly into hers, penetrating the net as if it did not exist.

She caught her breath sharply and stood transfixed. Her limbs felt heavy, incapable of movement, and she could not tear her eyes away from his. How long he held her bound she could not tell. It might have been seconds—minutes—or aeons of time. Then abruptly he turned, dropped into the driving seat of the Rover, the door slammed on him, the engine purred into life, and the brake lights winked derisively at her as it turned the corner of the stable block and sought the main road.

She shivered convulsively. It was like coming round from a trance. And the awakening brought a sensation as of intense cold, that reached out to encompass her from the twin icebergs that were his eyes, set in the unrelenting hardness of his face.

And now she had to go with him in the car to the hospital. Her heart leapt at the prospect, while her mind shrank from the ordeal. If only Willy would come, too! But Willy, for once, was remaining behind. To write out more reports? Or perhaps to interview more people while she, Marion, was conveniently out of the way? Was that why Reeve had suggested they remain away for lunch, and come back to Fallbeck at their leisure afterwards? She had wondered at his magnanimity at the time.

'He's got every move mapped out in advance,' she muttered with reluctant admiration. And at each move he was at least one step ahead of her, she admitted.

'I know someone who'll be thankful when your ankle's better.' Mrs Pugh rubbed the collie's ears, sympathetically, and to Marion's chagrin her smile included Reeve in the conversation as he emerged from the dining room after breakfast. 'Gyp's lost without his regular morning walk. I take him myself, but I don't go so far nor so fast as Marion,' she explained ruefully, 'and he's got used to being taken out first thing, wet or fine, ever since she came back. Oh well,' she told the disconsolate collie, 'you'll have to put up with it for a day or two longer yet. And to think;' she shook her head disbelievingly, 'when you took him out the other morning, all I worried about was you getting a wetting, and you ended up with your foot all bandages!'

Mrs Pugh did not know the full story of how she had come to hurt herself. When Reeve brought her back to the Fleece, Marion had merely said she'd sprained her ankle on the hill, and she had not seen fit to enlarge on her explanation since then. Neither, it seemed, had Reeve. She supposed she should feel grateful to him for that. She stole a glance at his face. He had accused her of going out to meet Ben Wade. . . .

'I saw no reason to worry Uncle and Mrs Pugh unnecessarily.' She spoke defensively the moment the car started, and they gained the road, and privacy to speak out of earshot of the housekeeper.

'There's no sense in worrying them,' he agreed evenly. 'If they knew what really happened, they'd be frightened out of their minds for you. Just as I . . . .' He broke off, and braked to let a cyclist go past.

'What time's your appointment at the hospital?' He set the car in motion again, and changed the subject at the same time.

'Nine-thirty.' They were conversing like strangers. Why did the cyclist have to appear and take his attention, just at that moment? What did he mean, 'just as I . . .'? Just as he would have been frightened, if he had been in her uncle's shoes? But he was not, she thought drearily. Reeve had not been worried about her, only angry that she had taken his time when he wanted to make another survey of the valley. She lapsed into silence. No doubt when he had the four women from the village in the car yesterday, they found plenty to talk about. She would have liked to ask him about them. Where had they gone? And why? But the words would not come. She would not give him the satisfaction of showing curiosity.

'I can walk.'

He did not argue with her, nor did he attempt to pick

her up. One part of her was glad; the other mourned the lack of his closeness, the feel of his arms around her. She stepped out carefully beside him, thankful that she had only a slight limp left, and she did not need to lower her pride to ask Reeve's help, but silently grateful that he had parked the car near enough to the Casualty Department entrance to ensure she had only a few steps to walk.

'It's coming along nicely,' the doctor pronounced his approval. 'I'll put another bandage on it for support. Keep it strapped up for another two or three days, and use it gently, and you should have no further trouble.'

She did not expect to—at least, not with her ankle. Reeve was an entirely different proposition, she thought with increasing exasperation, as he plied her with lunch at a nearby hotel afterwards, and throughout the meal kept up an easy conversation as if they had been chance-met acquaintances. She followed his lead, pride would not allow her to do otherwise, and somehow she ate her lunch in spite of the growing misery inside her that seemed to stop her throat from swallowing properly, and made the food itself taste as if it was sawdust—a slanderous description for the perfectly cooked meal that under other circumstances she would have partaken of with enthusiasm.

The talk ranged over her work—not his, she noticed, and her exasperation increased at his reticence—her uncle's book, travel and music, and to all outward appearances they were on the best of terms. They discovered a shared taste in music that could have been a link between them, Marion thought miserably, but the mutual liking seemed only to drive them further apart, since it brought no melting of the cold barrier which Reeve had presented to her since he kissed her yesterday, and from behind which he treated her with the impersonal politeness of a stranger. It hurt with a pain far sharper than she had yet known. Even quarrelling with him was better than this.

The conversation was brittle, unreal, and it seemed to Marion to go on and on, until her nerves were stretched to breaking point, and she longed to cry out to him,

'Stop it! Stop it!' Open hostility would have been easier to bear. But instead she ate her fruit and ice cream, and drank her coffee as if nothing untoward was happening, and agreed that she did not mind when he told her he intended to return to the Fleece via Merevale.

'I've got a call to make there, and it'll save another journey if I go on the way back.'

He did not say what the call was about, or on whom, and she did not ask. No doubt it furthered his plan to keep her away from Fallbeck for that much longer, and so delay her phoning round to find out who he had been to see, and what he had said. She settled back in the car seat, hoping he would assume her quietness was caused by tiredness. She closed her eyes and lay back, wishing Willy was there to break the silence that lay like a deep well between them.

It was shattered by a mechanical cacophony that sat Marion abruptly upright in her seat. Her eyes flew open in startled questioning and she felt the car slow down.

'Merevale Council's answer to progress,' Reeve said drily, and braked as a bulldozer slewed across the road and trundled away among the purposeful chaos of what appeared to be a new housing estate.

'Extra council houses, in Merevale? Whatever for?' Marion glanced about her curiously.

'An influx into the population, presumably.'

'There aren't all that many.' Marion could see the extent of the small development without moving from her seat.

'Twenty in all, including bungalows,' Reeve informed her casually, and she gave him a quick look.

'You seem to know a lot about them.'

'I told you, I make it my business to know these things,' he answered her blandly.

'The houses at the end are almost finished.' She leaned forward, interested in spite of herself. 'Look, those two have got bungalows attached to them. Almost like an annexe.'

'The jargon is "granny houses", I believe.'

'What a sensible idea.' She viewed the novel accommodation with approval. 'Ideal for someone with elderly parents—they could live close, and still have their own home.'

'That's the general idea.'

She shot him a suspicious look. Was he being sarcastic? But his face was devoid of expression as he went on,

'At least here they can allow a generous amount of garden to each house.' He pointed to two semi-detached blocks at the end, which already had their plots of land neatly fenced in. 'They'd be the envy of a good many private developments further south with that amount of room available. They've got a bus service, too.' He waited patiently while a single-decker coach disgorged a small crowd of passengers, before rumbling past them in the direction of Dale End.

'Hello, Mr Harland, have you come to take a look round?'

A square-looking man, shorter than Reeve, and incongruously dressed in a formal navy blue lounge suit and a fluorescent orange tin helmet, above a face that had a distinct air of authority about it, came over to the open window on Reeve's side of the car. Marion nodded recognition to his greeting; he was a local building contractor, and a member of Merevale District Council, and she knew him slightly, though not well.

'Not today,' Reeve shook his head.

Which implied he had been there before, for that purpose. Marion sent him an alert look, but he either did not notice, or chose to ignore it, because he went on, 'we're on our way to see Dick Blythe. We only stopped to give right of way to one of your bulldozers,' he smiled, 'it's bigger than we are.'

'In that case, I'm glad it stopped you,' the other returned.

'Why, was there something you wanted?' Reeve leaned back in his seat as if he had got all the time in the world, and Marion felt a surge of irritation. It suited him to keep her away from Fallbeck for as long as possible while Willy was engaged in carrying on the work he started the day before. And he had not told her he was going to see Dick Blythe. What business could he have with the farmer? she wondered. Surely he had not got his eye on Merevale, as well as the Fallbeck valley? The farm was the one Ben Wade bought his sheep from, the one Gyp had come from. She could not think what might take Reeve there, it seemed unlikely the two men were friends, it would be too much of a coincidence. Unless.... A thought struck her. Reeve might be interested in antiques. Dick Blythe was selling his holding and moving to a smaller house, and it was possible that some of his furniture might interest a collector.

'Only to let you know I've sent off that letter we were talking about,' the helmeted newcomer answered mysteriously, with a guarded look at Marion. She turned to look out of the window on her side of the car, pretending disinterest, but her ears pricked curiously. 'The recipient should find the offer very satisfactory,' he added discreetly.

What offer did he mean? Her alerted senses tingled. Was someone at Fallbeck already losing their nerve and selling out? She burned with indignation at the mere possibility.

'I suppose you don't know yet when the public enquiry is likely to be held?' the man asked.

'Within a day or two now,' Reeve answered, and Marion stiffened. He must be very sure of himself to contemplate such an early date.

'You've had the go-ahead from the local authority, then?' the man pressed interestedly, and Marion held her breath.

'Yes, I phoned them yesterday. They've accepted my report without reservations,' Reeve answered him quietly, and she let her breath out again with a small hiss, like the escape of steam through a safety valve, only this did nothing to relieve the pressure that was building up inside her, and threatened to explode if it did not find an outlet.

'You'll have a fight on your hands,' the Merevale councillor warned.

'Not too hard a one, I think,' Reeve answered with calm assurance. 'I only expect really serious opposition from the one quarter.'

At least he had the good sense to recognise her potential as an opponent, Marion thought with quick triumph.

'And with the right handling, it shouldn't be too difficult to overcome,' he added confidently.

Her face flamed. What did he mean, the right handling? Manlike, he probably thought a few kisses in the firelight would be enough to overcome any opposition he might encounter from her. With shame, she remembered her surrender the day before. But that was yesterday. Today, she felt strong enough to meet him on his own terms again, and Reeve would discover her opposition to be more serious than he expected, she determined. She began to look forward to the public enquiry. There at least she would have a chance to speak her mind, perhaps sway those who were teetering on the edge of indecision, as she felt sure she could have swayed them at the meeting in the bar-room, if only Reeve had not arrived.

'I suppose you mean the Wade family?' the councillor guessed resignedly.

'I mean the Wade family,' Reeve confirmed, and his lips tilted in a slight grin.

Marion stared at him in open-mouthed astonishment. He completely discounted any opposition she might offer, with deflating casualness, brushing her away, she thought angrily, as he might brush at a persistent mosquito, which he found irritating, but ineffective, and without a second thought he concentrated on where he expected the real opposition to come from. The Wade family. Her colour receded as quickly as it rose, leaving her with a frozen pallor that matched the icy fury inside her.

She was scarcely conscious of the car beginning to move again. Scarcely conscious of the tin-helmeted man's cheerful, "Bye for now,' although she heard her own voice automatically responding, and wondered how it was that she could still observe surface courtesies without showing anything of the near-erupting volcano of her feelings.

'It looks as if Dick Blythe's got visitors.' Reeve broke the taut silence between them as he carefully eased the car round the last bend of a track of teeth-rattling roughness, and crawled to a halt in the farmyard close to where men were loading sheep into a high-sided lorry. One was Dick Blythe himself, the retiring owner of the farm. The other two—she caught her breath—were Aaron Wade and Ben.

'The opposition,' murmured Reeve interestedly.

'Only two of them,' Marion corrected him sharply. She would not be dismissed so lightly. Deliberately she opened the door on her side of the car and swung out to join Reeve as he strolled towards the group of men beside the lorry. He gave her a long look, but he made no comment, and she stuck close to his side. Whatever he said to Dick Blythe or to the Wades, she meant to be there to hear it, whether he regarded it as her business or not.

'Hello, Mr Harland. I'm glad you've turned up, I've just been having a word with Aaron and Ben here.' The white-haired farmer turned to Reeve with every appearance of relief, as if he had not found the exchange of words a cordial one.

'It's no good you trying to get round me. I've told tha' the same as I've told him,' Aaron Wade jerked a not over-clean thumb in Reeve's direction. 'No!' he growled, and gave an angry thwack with his stick at a wily ewe which tried to dodge round his legs and evade the circling dog. 'Get up!' he snarled, and the animal clattered up the wooden ramp to the lorry, giving a lead to the huddle of sheep that the collie was trying to drive in the same direction.

'That's what you're trying to do to us,' Marion turned on Reeve bitterly. 'Drive us like sheep, in the direction you want us to go. And I suppose if we don't all conform you'll lash out, the same as he did.' She did not bother to lower her voice. Aaron Wade's stick had fallen unnecessarily hard,

and her flashing eyes made her disapproval plain, but her
outspoken criticism served only to inflame the farmer's
already unstable temper, and he snarled,

'Here's one as won't be driven, whether tha' likes it or
not.' He sent an angry look at Reeve.

'Now, Dad, if you'd just listen....'

Marion stared at Ben in astonishment. Surely Reeve
had not been able to talk the youth round to his way of
thinking as well? It did not seem possible.

'I'm not going to listen to anything he's got to say,'
Aaron Wade jerked his head at Reeve in a furious gesture.

'I didn't say listen to him,' Ben placated hurriedly,
'but you could listen to Dick Blythe here. You must know
what he said makes sense.'

'He's only trying to get rid of his holding.'

'I've already sold my farm,' Dick Blythe interjected, with
the air of one who is rapidly running out of patience. 'And
if I'd got any sense I'd let you take the sheep and go your
own stubborn way,' he said tersely. 'It's to my advantage to
let you have them, but don't complain when they lose
condition, as they will on the grazing the Fallbeck valley
has to offer,' he predicted.

'They'll do well enough.' Aaron Wade was surly.

'Well enough, yes, particularly on the summer grass, but
they'll not look like they do now, by this time next year,'
their former owner warned. 'They're a bigger strain than
the hill sheep you run, and they need better quality feeding.
And from what I know of your sheepwalks, they give
sparse keep, and they're over-grazed already,' he added
drily.

'They'll cope with all I want to put on them,' Aaron
Wade retorted. He reached down for a corner of the
heavy wooden ramp which also served as a door to close
the end of the lorry, and lifted it with a quick jerk of his
powerful arms, scarcely giving the collie time to jump
clear before he slammed it shut on the last of the sheep.
He speeded the dog's retreat with an impatient curse and
turned with the steel peg in his hand ready to drop it in

place to secure the barrier, as Dick Blythe spoke again.

'You can't have all that much grazing to spare, or you wouldn't have tried to take over the sheepwalks on my land where it adjoins yours,' he observed shrewdly.

'Who told you that?' Aaron Wade shouted angrily. 'I suppose it was him?' referring to Reeve.

Marion listened to the interchange with increasing puzzlement. There was an undercurrent here she did not understand, a link between the three men which she could not place.

'He was instrumental in selling my farm for me, so he had to know,' Dick Blythe answered her one question, and posed another. Why did Reeve want the farm? Surely he was not thinking of settling down there himself?

'I've brought the signed letter of intent.' Reeve reached into his breast pocket and pulled out his wallet. 'Although it's not strictly necessary now, because the contract's been signed, and your copy will be in your hands by tomorrow morning's post.' He extracted an envelope and held it out to the farmer, who took it with a nod of thanks and started to speak, only to be interrupted by Aaron Wade's roar of anger.

'So it was you who blocked my way to getting extra land? You....'

His action was deliberate, Marion felt sure. Her horror-struck eyes registered it like a slow-motion movie, although in fact it was all over within a split second.

With a furious exclamation the enraged man slung away the steel peg in his hand, and with a quick jerk he pulled the heavy ramp from against the back of the lorry. Once started on the downward swing, its own weight did the rest. Marion heard Ben shout, 'Dad, don't!' Saw the quick jerk of the man's arm as he sent the barrier crashing down, and heard her own voice cry, 'Reeve, look out!'

Reeve glanced round, and his reaction was instantaneous. His quicksilver leap saved him from catching the full force of the heavy wooden ramp, but even so the side of it caught him a glancing blow, as it fell with a resounding crash to the ground.

A fraction of her mind registered the sudden rush of sheep down the ramp to freedom; felt the press of panicking woollen bodies getting in her way as she stumbled through them. Heard the collie give tongue, and Ben call out something to him, and then she was by Reeve's side. He lay on his face, his arms outstretched, and regardless of the others Marion dropped on to her knees in the dust of the yard, her trembling hands frantically seeking to turn him over.

'Reeve! Reeve, darling,' she sobbed. 'Oh God, don't let him be hurt, I can't bear it!' Tears streamed down her face, blinding her eyes, and she cradled him in her arms, stroking his hair, his face. 'Oh, Reeve, my heart, my love!' The salt of her own tears, wet on his forehead, stung her lips as she pressed them in anguished entreaty on his brow. Someone knelt on her other side, stiffly, as if getting down was an effort, and Dick Blythe's voice penetrated her distress, calm, soothing, and infinitely reassuring.

'It caught his shoulder, not his head. He'll not be badly hurt, I think.'

And then, unbelievably, Reeve stirred. She felt new life flow through his limbs, energise his body, and grasping her for support he sat up. Had he heard what she said? There was no way she could tell.

'Don't cry, Marion,' he spoke quietly, but his voice was strong, and firm. 'I'm only bruised. It floored me for a moment, that's all.' So he had not completely lost consciousness, which meant he must have heard her. And this time he must have known she was not acting a part. . . .

She sat back on her heels and looked at him, as if she could never look enough. It did not matter if he had heard her, understood what she said. She no longer cared. Her pride was gone, and nothing mattered now except that he was alive, unhurt. His face was chalk white, but her clearing vision saw that it was the pallor of anger rather than injury. She put out a tentative hand to help him as he got to his feet, but he gave a brief shake of his head, and she desisted and let her arm drop to her side again as he stood unaided, and began slowly to brush himself down.

'It were an accident....' Aaron Wade seemed to have shrunk. He shuffled towards Reeve, his eyes looking anywhere but at the man he had tried to injure, and all his bluff and bluster had vanished.

'Dad didn't mean it, Mr Harland.'

'He meant it, and you know it.' Reeve stopped brushing and straightened up, then looked at the father and son, and the quietness of his tone belied the steel that lay underneath. 'What's more, I've got two witnesses to prove it,' he went on, and nodded towards Dick Blythe and Marion, and his voice dripped ice.

'What'll you do?' Ben's voice was fearful.

'I'll have to consider what to do.' Reeve was uncompromising, and Marion felt almost sorry for the youth. She remembered Reeve's terms to herself: no quarter given on either side. 'Come on, Marion, I've delivered Dick's letter, there's no need for us to stay here any longer.'

'You've dropped your wallet, Mr Harland, don't go without it.'

'I'll pick it up,' Marion offered immediately. Dick Blythe's back was stiff with years, and she could reach the ground more easily than he could. Quickly she stooped and gathered up the scattered contents of the soft leather holdall. A bankers' card—business cards—a gold-embossed one said, 'Harland and Son, Contractors,' so it was Reeve's own firm he worked for. His own, and his father's. She put the card back in its place. The knowledge did not matter any longer. It seemed totally unimportant beside the last item she picked up from the dust of the yard, and replaced with infinite care in the fold of the wallet from where it had fallen.

She knew it had come from there, because the imprint of it still remained in the fine leather. The imprint of a rosebud. An old-fashioned tea rose, plucked from the walled garden behind the Fleece. The same bud, she felt sure, that Reeve had worn in the lapel of his jacket the first night of his stay with them, from the vase full she had picked, and put in his room.

She handled it tenderly, and surreptitiously pressed it to her lips before she gently replaced it and closed the wallet. And looked up to find Reeve was watching her, his gaze probing her face. He saw her action, saw she had recognised the bud for what it was, and—she caught her breath, and her eyes searched his face—why had he kept it there? And she knew, with absolute certainty, that he had heard and understood every word she spoke while he lay on the ground.

CHAPTER FOURTEEN

The public enquiry was over in a much shorter time than Marion would have believed possible.

She did not see Reeve on his own again, after they left the farm, and before the meeting began. Dick Blythe overrode his protestations that he was perfectly capable of driving, and insisted on taking over the wheel on their return journey, although Reeve firmly rejected any suggestion that he should visit the hospital on the way back and have his injured shoulder attended to.'

'I should know if there was anything broken.'

'You made me go.' Fear for him made Marion angry.

'That was different.'

'How like a man!'

She subsided into the back seat of the car, simmering with silent resentment. But if she argued, he might reject Dick Blythe's offer to drive them back, and do more harm than good, and she dared not risk that happening, however much she wished they could be on their own. If the farmer had not been with them, Reeve might have explained the presence of the rosebud in his wallet. Again, he might not, and then her agony of indecision would have been even worse.

'I can't understand Aaron Wade,' Dick Blythe kept up a running conversation while he drove. 'He always was a stubborn man, but to have someone offer him a good price for the poor sort of holding he farms, and replace it with a place that's more fertile, and more profitable, even if it isn't much bigger—well, I reckon he must be out of his mind,' he ejaculated disgustedly.

So that was Reeve's connection with Dick Blythe's farm. He had not bought it for himself, but as an inducement to entice Aaron Wade to move.

'It wouldn't take much to win young Ben over,' the retiring farmer opined. 'He's not a bad sort, for all he takes after his father with his awkward ways. I reckon he can see the chance of a better return for his work if they take over my place, and there'd be a bit more company for him in Merevale at the end of the day, too.'

'What about Zilla Wade?' Reeve questioned.

'She'd move like a shot, if you ask me,' Dick Blythe answered without hesitation. 'She's duty bound to uphold her husband, of course,' he added sagely, 'but what woman wouldn't exchange an old-fashioned, tumbledown farmhouse, miles from anywhere, and with no modern conveniences to speak of, for a place like mine that's built next the lane, and within reach of a bus service. The house has been modernised inside with electric light and running hot and cold water too, and I hear they're bringing the gas out to those new council houses they're building, so that'll be another facility Merevale will have to offer, if they want it. It's Aaron you've got to convince, not his family,' their self-appointed chauffeur concluded not very hopefully.

'He's just given me a lever that might help me to do just that,' said Reeve, and rubbed his bruised shoulder with a thoughtful hand, and once again Marion saw the heavy wooden ramp crashing down. Would Reeve use the

threat of reprisals for his action against Aaron Wade to
force him to agree to the exchange of farms, and so clear
the last serious obstacle from the path of the reservoir?

She had no opportunity to ask him. The moment they
stopped on the forecourt of the Fleece Willy hastened out
of the door to meet them and whisked Reeve away without
preliminary.

'You're wanted at a Council meeting this evening, and
a joint meeting with the water authorities tomorrow
morning. You'll just have time to make it, if you go right
away.'

Reeve turned to wave as Willy drove him away, but
her uncle and Mrs Pugh were standing on the step beside
her, to see them off, so she could not regard his gesture as
being especially for her benefit.

He was gone for two days, each of which seemed like a
lifetime to Marion. The phone rang and she fled to answer
it, but it was Willy on the end of the line, not Reeve.

'He asked me to let your uncle know about the public
enquiry meeting. Miles promised to let him have a room
for the purpose.'

Marion took down the details with numb disappointment. If only Reeve himself had rung! There was no reason
why he should, except the inexplicable presence of a tiny
cream rosebud, pressed into the soft leather of his wallet,
which he took from the inside top pocket of his jacket—
the pocket next to his heart.

'Reeve's still stuck at that meeting with the Council
people and the Water Authority officials,' Willy's cheerful
voice informed her. 'Rather him than me. It's been going
on for hours.'

'When do you expect to be back?'

'The day after tomorrow, in time for the public enquiry.
We'll be coming with the people who are at the meeting
now.'

'Saturday, about four o'clock.' Marion took down the
details mechanically, as she would take any ordinary booking for rooms at the hotel.

Another day and a half before she saw Reeve again. And then he would be with a party of strangers. The time stretched like an eternity before her. She took Gyp for a walk, but she dared not go far for fear of over-straining her ankle. And besides, while she was away, Reeve might ring.

He did not, and she wandered restlessly to her studio and started to work on her woodcut, but she could not concentrate, and gave it up with a sigh of impatience, and wandered restlessly back again to stare out of the window at the perpetually empty road, along which Reeve would not come until the day after tomorrow.

All time passes, however slowly, and eventually Saturday afternoon arrived, and with it Reeve and Willy. Half a dozen other men were with them, sober-suited and carrying briefcases, obviously representatives of the interested authorities, but Marion saw and heard only Reeve.

She heard him speak, even before he came through the door. The party of men were all talking at once, but Reeve's voice reached her through the general babble of conversation, clear and distinct, like a clarion call, and her heart raced. Suddenly, now he was here, she felt nervous. Had she read too much into the fact that he carried one of the rose-buds she picked for his room? Her aunt had been a keen gardener, wont to take cuttings of plants that took her fancy and then forget about them, and find them about her person when they were dried and wilted and usually beyond saving so far as getting them to grow was concerned. Per-haps Reeve was like that? He had mentioned he was fond of roses, and the bush that grew in the walled garden was an old-fashioned variety, with a particularly sweet perfume, that would probably be unobtainable from a nursery now. Perhaps he kept the bud to remind him to ask for a cutting before he left the Fleece?

Then the door opened and Reeve stood there. He seemed to dwarf the other men in the party. He had on the same steel grey suit that he wore the first evening he was with them, but this time—her eyes flew to his jacket lapel—

there was no rosebud there. She knew a sense of sickening disappointment, which was ridiculous because the roses in the walled garden were over now until their second blooming in the autumn, but his jacket lapel looked bare without the bud, empty—as empty as her heart felt, in its confusion and uncertainty.

She raised her eyes to his face, but she could not read the expression there in the subdued light of the low-ceilinged hall. He had seen her. His eyes swept the hall when he came in and rested on her where she stood against the stairs. She caught her breath, and her heart thudded until she was certain he must hear it. He moved, as if he might come towards her, and her hand rose to her throat to still the wildly throbbing pulse that beat there until it felt as if it would choke her. Then one of the other men in the party spoke to Reeve, asked him a question, and he turned aside to answer it, while Marion leaned back against the newel post of the stairway, drained and shaken as if she had been driven by a mighty storm.

She watched in a daze as he disappeared with the rest of the party into the room prepared for the meeting, and Jim the barman propped open the outside door to give easy access to the steady stream of people who began to arrive to join them. A buffet table had been prepared at the back of the room, with a huge urn of tea supervised by Mrs Pugh, and Marion slipped on to a chair near the door as the meeting began. One of the strangers chaired it, and stilled the buzz of talk by his brief opening preamble, only to set it off again by his straightforward invitation for the people present to voice their objections to the proposed reservoir plan, or to put any questions they might have regarding Reeve's discussions with them, and the offers he had made.

Marion listened with a sense of growing unreality as the meeting progressed. There were few serious objections, not even, she realised with surprise, from Aaron Wade, who sat between his wife and son in subdued silence. Reeve had done his work well. The compensation he offered must have been very good, or the reasons he put forward for the people concerned to move home overriding, to have such an effect on a gathering which Marion had anticipated would be stormy, to say the least.

She felt no bitterness at Reeve's success, not even when, by an adroit remark, he prevented her from taking any effective part in the discussion. The Chairman's glance roved round the room, seeking someone to make the first contribution, and his eye stopped at Marion.

'Miss Dorman?' he invited.

'Miss Dorman is only in Fallbeck on a prolonged visit to relatives,' Reeve put in before she could speak. 'She's not a permanent resident.'

A small spark of rebellion glowed inside her for a moment, then it died down, and she made a hopeless gesture and shook her head. She could not fight any more, because it meant fighting Reeve, and she made no comment when the Chairman said,

'In that case, Miss Dorman's interest can only be academic,' and he passed on to the next nearest.

She listened to them all with a sort of detached wonder.

The postmistress. 'I've got to go and live in Dale End anyway. Our Brenda's having her third, and she's written to say she can't manage on her own.'

And John Cornish. He had lost his haunted look, she realised suddenly, and seemed relaxed, and somehow eager. 'I've received an offer to second the headmaster at Merevale school for the last eighteen months until I retire. It came out of the blue, and it's much too good an offer to refuse.'

It had not come out of the blue, Marion thought shrewdly, remembering the remark made by the councillor in the orange tin helmet. Reeve had had a hand in this. Showing that after all, he cared, for the people of the valley as well as for his reservoir. A small, warm spot touched her frozen heart at the thought, an oasis of comfort in her desert of uncertainty.

The wife of one of the quarrymen, one of the two brothers who looked after their father's holding as well as doing their own jobs during the day, finally summed up the general feeling when she said,

'Well, you can do what you please, but we've accepted one of those houses with a bungalow attached. It'll give Dad a bit of garden to keep him happy, our men will be nearer to their work, and the children will be able to go to school without the dread of being boarded out with strangers every winter, once they're over eleven years old. And my friends are coming too, for that reason,' she nodded to the mothers of the two sets of twins.

'That really only leaves Mr Wade to comment,' the chairman said mildly, with a questioning look at Aaron.

It left her uncle as well, Marion thought, and wondered why that did not rouse her. She should be battling for him, for the Fleece, but he had sat at the side of the room close to Mrs Pugh, and remained silent throughout the whole of the meeting. Neither he nor the housekeeper offered to say a word. She was about to speak up, whether Reeve wanted her to or not, when Zilla Wade shrilled to her husband,

'Well, say your piece!' She nudged a reluctant Aaron to his feet, and when he did not immediately comply she administered a further prod which drove him into speech.

'I ain't got no objections,' he muttered unwillingly, but clearly enough for all to hear. 'The arrangement we came to is O.K with me.' And he sat down again hurriedly, leaving his wife and son with satisfied smiles on their faces, which confirmed Dick Blythe's guess that they, at least, were more than ready to exchange farms, and Marion's suspicion that Reeve had brought pressure to bear on Aaron that he dared not resist in view of his recent dangerous lapse of behaviour.

'Who'd have thought all this would have happened, and in such a short time, too?'

Rose, their daily help, collected cups of tea for herself and her husband as the meeting broke up into chattering groups, and turned cheerfully to greet Reeve as he strolled across the room to join them.

'The day .I spilled your papers out of that slippy plastic folder thing, and had to take them in to Miss Marion to put them right again for you ... here, have my cup of tea, I haven't drunk out of it, I'll get myself another.' With hardly a pause for breath Rose pressed her refreshment on Reeve, helped herself from the urn, and carried on talking. 'And then I came back upstairs with your hanky, you know, the one you put round Miss Marion's wrist where she'd cut herself, and heard you both quarrelling about the reservoir. Well, I said to my husband here, when he got home that night, who'd have thought it? I said.'

'It caused quite a stir,' her husband remembered with a grin. 'We'd got a houseful that night, too, being our son's eighteenth birthday, and they were all valley folk there. It made them prick their ears up, I can tell you.'

Marion looked straight at Reeve. She met his eyes, and her own were unflinching. For the first time since she had known Rose she felt glad of her garrulous tongue.

'I didn't break my promise,' she told him quietly. Even if she never saw him again after tonight, it was important he should know she had not broken her promise to him to keep silent about his plans.

'I know.'

Rose turned to greet a crony, pulling her husband with her, and Reeve and Marion were alone. In the crowded room, with a press of chattering people around them, she felt as if they were on a desert island. The grey of his eyes was the cool water surrounding them, tempting her to immerse in their clear depths. She drew a long, shuddering breath.

'I never seriously thought you did,' he went on, equally quietly. 'I was angry at the time. Will you forgive me?'

What had she got to forgive him for? It was all over now. She started to speak, but other people invaded the solitude of their island. People who, now the meeting was over, wanted to go home and attend to other things. The Council men and the Water Authority officials closed their briefcases and came over to shake hands with Reeve, congratulating him on a mission successfully accomplished, and then they, too, left, and besides herself and Reeve there were only Miles Dorman and Mrs Pugh.

'You didn't say anything at the meeting.' Belatedly Marion remembered her uncle's puzzling silence. 'What about the Fleece?' she asked him.

'We don't really want it any more.' Miles Dorman dismissed his hotel with calm indifference. 'Stella and I have decided to go and live in Dale End,' he smiled across at his housekeeper. 'We intend to be married quietly....'

Married? Stella? Marion felt her senses whirl. With a vague feeling of astonishment she realised this was the first time she had heard Mrs Pugh's Christian name.

'Your uncle will have access to a good library to help him with his writing,' the housekeeper's calm voice brought her back to earth again. 'There's a place for sale within easy walking distance of the library, and we've been given the first option. It's got a bit of orchard and paddock attached, so there'll be space enough for Gyp to run, and no chance of him getting into mischief among the sheep.'

'Congratulations!' Reeve brought her to her senses, and a sense of what was expected of her.

'I'm so glad. I'd no idea....' She flung her arms round her uncle, then round Mrs Pugh. She was glad for them. She only wished her heart would not cry so loudly. 'If only it was me!'

'The young are curiously blind,' Miles Dorman observed in his gentle voice. 'Come, my dear. Rose will clear up in here for you.' And he armed Mrs Pugh—no, Stella, thought Marion half hysterically—out of the door, and back to their own private quarters.

'And then there were two.'

He had said that before. Only this time she did not feel afraid. Her arms rose as he clasped her closely to him, and she ran soft fingertips through his hair, tracing the line of it where it curled into the nape of his neck, while her lips responded hungrily to his kisses.

'I love you. I love you,' he murmured, and never had her ears heard a sweeter sound. 'Tell me you love me—again,' he begged, and his eyes were dark with the intensity of his feeling.

'I told you when I thought you were unconscious,' a light of happy teasing lit her eyes. 'I tried to tell you, that day at the waterfall,' she remembered it as if it was another lifetime. 'You wouldn't let me speak. You shouted at me, in the helicopter.' She drew his head down closer to her own, and forgave him with her lips.

'I was terrified,' he confessed softly. 'I knew you'd fallen over the edge of the waterfall, and I couldn't find you. I thought I'd never see you again.'

He smoothed hands that suddenly trembled across her pale gold hair, and his lips became urgent with remembered fear, parting her own, but tenderly, seeking, pleading, fired by her response with a passionate urgency that would not be denied.

'You kept your rosebud.'

When his lips became weary at last, she leaned her head against his shoulder, and remembered the empty lapel.

'I kept it because it reminded me of you.' He traced an exploring finger against the softly rounded outline of her cheek, stroking the delicate bloom that glowed under his touch with the rose of happiness.

'How long have you known?' She turned glowing eyes to his.

'From the time I first saw you on the fellside,' he confessed. 'Why else do you think I followed you home, to see where you went, then dragged Willy all the way out here to stay at the Fleece, just so that I could get to know you?'

'You didn't tell me.' If only she had known! But she knew now, and that was all that mattered.

'I thought you'd hate me, because of the reservoir.'

'I tried to tell myself I did.'

'You told me you loved me, when you thought I couldn't hear. Bless Aaron Wade and his lorry ramp,' he said contentedly, and smilingly kissed the soft, shy flush that deepened the rose of her cheeks, and traced with his lips the curve of her downbent lashes.

'When will you marry me?' he demanded, and tipped gentle fingers under her chin, turning her face up to his.

'Soon. Let it be soon.'

'It'll mean travelling, because of my work.' His face clouded suddenly. 'I couldn't bear us to be parted.'

'I'll come with you, wherever you go.' She would go to the ends of the earth, with Reeve.

'I love you so,' he groaned, and strained her to him with a passionate embrace, holding her close against his heart, while he buried his face in the gold, silky mane of her hair, and Marion closed her eyes, and gave herself up to a moment that would l.   for them both, for ever.

The lowering sun peeped benignly through the windows, tinting all it touched with gold. It smiled on the two figures, now blended into one, and sent their soft shadow across the carpeted room. And they were both too preoccupied to notice that the shadow lay behind them.

What readers say about Harlequin Romances

"Harlequins take away the world's troubles and for a while you can live in a world of your own where love reigns supreme."

"Thank you for bringing romance back to me."

"I find Harlequins are the only stories on the market that give me a satisfying romance with sufficient depth without being maudlin."

"Harlequins are magic carpets...away from pain and depression...away to other people and other countries one might never know otherwise."

Harlequin Romances

The books that let you escape
into the wonderful world of romance!
Trips to exotic places... interesting
plots... meeting memorable people...
the excitement of love.... These are
integral parts of Harlequin Romances —
the heartwarming novels read by
women everywhere.

Many early issues are now available.
Choose from this great selection!

Choose from this list of Harlequin Romance editions.*

*Some of these book were originally published under different titles.